Survivor Max II:

School Bites

by

Davi Barker

Book Two in the Survivor Max Series

PrepperPress

Your Survival Library

www.PrepperPress.com

Survivor Max II: School Bites

ISBN 978-1-939473-31-8
Copyright © 2015 by Davi Barker

Printed in the United States of America.

Prepper Press Paperback Edition: October 2015
Prepper Press is a division of Kennebec Publishing, LLC

About the Author

A lifelong fan of the undead, Davi Barker believes that art should imitate life, and if it can't it should at least imitate the living dead. Inspired by the big lurkers and shakers in the zombie genre, Davi aims to really flesh out the metaphor of the flesh eaters. Zombies are unique among monsters because they outnumber the living, which enacts one of literature's most enduring themes: the triumph of the individual over the collective. And as the dead escape their graves to consume the living, it is the survivors who must build the new world in the shell of the old.

Special thanks to John Mendes, author of
Cote ci Cote la: Trinidad & Tobago Dictionary
for his invaluable help creating the voice of Moses.
(www.cotecicotela.com)

Dear Survivors,

This is Lochshire Estates, where I grew up. You probably think it looks pretty secure. Concrete walls provide quite a bit of protection from the infected, but before you move in, you should know what happened here. As far as I know, I'm the only Lochshire resident who survived. I escaped with my new friend, Ellie, from Boston, and my neighbor's cat, Stinky Romero.

I'm Max Hartwell. My dad was Rich Hartwell, a scientist who was researching the Walking Hunger virus. If you're looking for him, you're too late, but before we lost power, I printed out his research. If I can find someone who gets it, maybe we can find a cure.

Don't be surprised if you can't find any weapons or ammo here. Guns were banned in the housing agreement, so we improvised. Don't go in the pool, and don't open the west tower's dumpster room. There are infected inside.

We took all the food and gear we could carry, but we left the rest in apartment 4D in the east tower. Be careful! There was a herd on the south side when we left. The safest entrance is probably the front door on the tower's west side. We cleared that out as best as we could.

We're headed to Thornton Middle School. I was a student there. Right after the outbreak, the police turned it into a refugee center, but it was overrun weeks ago. It's probably not safe there, but we need medicine. Ellie has a nasty gash. It's not a bite, but we can't risk an infection.

If you stay here, the first thing to do is fix the front gate. We had to rip it out to escape. It's straight ahead, wedged against the entrance of the south tower. Be careful! There were about fifty creepers inside when we left. One of them was the Postman.

The Postman is different. It's smarter than the others, and they sense it. They follow it like a leader. A doctor on the radio said that some of the infected are smarter because they were aggressive people before. The disease keeps whatever it can use, and destroys the rest, so it keeps the aggressive parts of the brain.

We're not coming back here. Dad had a cabin on the south side of Stinson Lake, ten miles southwest of here. The cabin is secluded, and safe. It should be well-supplied. We'll wait out the winter there. All peaceful survivors are free to join us. But if you're hostile, I'm warning you to stay away. We'll have weapons and won't hesitate to defend our property.

If you stay in Lochshire, I hope you can make more of this place than we could.

Don't get bit,

Survivor Max

Chapter One: All Downhill from Here

The gray clouds were so thick I couldn't tell what time it was, only that we were losing daylight. It looked like a storm was taking shape. We were due for the first snow, and it certainly felt cold enough.

My poncho was reinforced with duct tape to protect against bites, so rather than digging through my gear bag for the roll, I just pulled a piece off my sleeve and taped the letter to the ruins of the front gate. I'd also fashioned myself a utility belt out of duct tape that held my multi-tool, a hammer, Ellie's hatchet, my dad's handheld two-way radio, and some other small gear. My helmet was made from a spaghetti strainer, with my LED headlamp attached to it. All my other supplies were stuffed in my bag.

Ellie had my other radio. I was eleven-years-old and she was maybe a year older than me at most. Her red hair was loose and untamed. She was sitting on the curb in a green hoodie, staring at the empty revolver on the pavement in front of her, still wiping tears from her eyes.

Ellie's mom was slumped on the ground between us. She'd been bitten, and turned. When it attacked me, Ellie had to shoot it. The .38 caliber slug entered its head just under the left eye, and was embedded in the hollow stump of a sugar maple tree across the street. It was our last bullet.

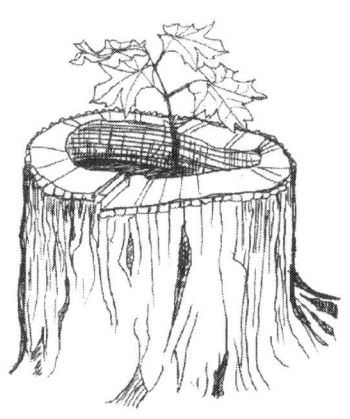

In the stump was a small, almost insignificant sapling. I'd always wanted to see a tree growing inside another tree, but in all the time I lived there, and all the seed pods I buried in that old stump, none had ever taken root. Strange that I'd finally get to see one grow there now. If it survived the harsh New Hampshire winter, and if I ever came back, maybe I'd get to see it. But I didn't have much hope for long-term plans.

The gunshot had drawn creepers out of the neighboring houses.

"We need to move," I said.

"You're right." She rummaged through her mom's rucksack for supplies, transferring a water bottle, a road map, and a handheld flashlight to her own book bag. "Let's get out of here." She holstered the revolver on her belt between her lock blade and a compact trifold shovel.

Ellie was sweating. I checked her bandage. Her ankle was red and swollen. "It's infected," I told her. "I have some ibuprofen in my med kit for the pain and fever, but we need to get you some antibiotics and fast."

"Don't you think you're overreacting? I've had worse," she said.

"Maybe, but there's no hospital. A serious blood infection is bad, like amputation bad. Like death bad."

She winced with pain when she put weight on her injured ankle. I helped her to her feet.

Stinky was a black and white tuxedo cat that I adopted after the collapse. In some ways, he had adopted me. His previous owner didn't fare so well, and even though he had been an indoor cat, he was going feral just as fast as we were. Vigilance was among his growing skills, and I'd learned to rely on his eyes and ears more than my own. He saw the first creeper headed our way before I did. The low groan he made when he saw a creeper was different than any other sound he ever made and I learned to recognize it. As soon as I heard him, I perked up.

I heard the creeper before I saw it, headed our way from a house down the hill. Its long wails would call others. It was a woman in a flannel shirt and denim overalls. The red stains on its face meant it had fed recently, and the gardening shears in its shoulder told me its meal had fought back. The uphill climb slowed it down, but we didn't have much time.

4

Ellie limped as the neighbor closed in. A small mail truck was parked in front of the compound. "That's our ticket out of here!" I whispered. It was unlocked, but there was only one seat, and no keys. I helped Ellie into the seat. "Stinky, up!" I slapped the side console and Stinky jumped up and meowed at me as if to say, *hurry!*

"Put it in neutral and steer," I told Ellie. "It's all downhill from here. I just need to get it rolling. We can coast the whole way, but we have to move fast."

She nodded. "Go! I got this." She put her hands on the wheel, looking determined as she scrunched her brow.

I ran to the back of the mail truck and pushed, but it wouldn't budge.

I heard a growl and Ellie screamed. It was a teenage creeper that must have come from the woods. It grabbed Ellie's hair through the window, and tried to pull her out. It turned as I came around, reaching for me with one hand and clutching Ellie with the other. Its lips were ripped off, its teeth dripping blood as it snarled. Flesh was missing from its fingertips, leaving the bones exposed. A perfect delivery system for infection.

I pulled the hatchet from my belt and swung, severing its jaw. The thing let go of Ellie as it collapsed, but it wasn't dead. I lifted the hatchet over my head and slammed it down into its skull.

I'd never killed one before, but it was no time to reflect. The gardening shears creeper was getting closer.

I looked in the window. Ellie was shaken, but adrenaline brought her to full attention. "Pull the emergency brake!" I pointed. She nodded and cranked up the window.

When she released the lever, the mail truck began rolling downhill on its own.

More creepers stumbled toward us from houses up the road, and they were moving fast. I got behind the mail truck and pushed with all my strength, to build speed. We had to move faster to outrun them.

I got it to walking speed, but the next creeper was only yards away, and catching up. I got it to running speed when suddenly Ellie swerved hard to the left, throwing me off my step.

"Incoming!" she screamed and hit the gardening sheers creeper. The rotting body went under the tires, and I hopped as it came out from under the back of the mail truck. The creeper behind me tripped over it, but more were coming.

I ran to catch up to the mail truck and jumped onto the back bumper. The next two creepers were a few feet away, so I unlatched the back and opened the roll door. I fell into a pile of undelivered mail.

A creeper grabbed the back bumper and held on, getting dragged behind the mail truck. I slammed the roll door down on its hands, but it still held on. On the third try I heard its hands crunch, and the door latched with the creature's fingers sticking out. I couldn't pull it open again. If the creeper was still attached, I'd deal with it later.

I poked my head in the cab. "I think we're clear. How are you doing up here?"

Ellie swerved to avoid more creepers. They chased us but we were too fast. "I'm good," she said.

"Want me to drive?"

"No, I got this. Give me those pain meds."

I grabbed a few pill packets from my first aid kit and offered her my water, but she swallowed them dry. "Now, where's this school of yours?"

"Down the hill, make a left at the bottom. Try not to hit any of them. We don't want to lose speed."

Stinky watched the creepers go by. In the side mirror, I saw at least six of them chasing us. They were falling behind, but they weren't giving up. We had to keep moving.

"That was close!" I leaned into the cab of the mail truck.

"Too close!" Ellie zigzagged between creepers in the road.

We couldn't start the engine, but what mattered was we were rolling faster than them. The mountain road snaked through the autumn trees and the midday chill was merciless. Ellie was skillfully downshifting and tapping the brake to slow us down and maintain control.

We passed cottages that were dark and still, like granite blocks sticking out of the wilderness. We passed a blue house, where a man had its face buried in the carcass of a large dog, squeezing the intestines into its mouth like toothpaste.

It looked up as we rolled by, got to its feet, and came after us.

"Is it like this everywhere?" I asked.

"Everywhere I've been," Ellie replied. "More or less. This isn't so bad. It's easy when they're spread out, not like in cities."

"The refugee center's gonna be bad, isn't it?"

"Let's search these houses for some ammo. I don't like being out here unarmed."

"No time. We have to get you antibiotics right away."

"There's probably all kinds of supplies in these houses. Food, car keys, maybe a shotgun. We'd probably find medicine, too."

"I guess it's possible, but prescription antibiotics aren't that common. We could waste all day searching and not find them. The refugee center is a sure thing."

"How do you know?"

"I saw the ambulances and the Health Department pull into my school on day one. Emergency broadcasts said to go there. It was overrun by creepers the first week. That means it's almost fully stocked."

"No. That means it was fully stocked weeks ago. You think you're the only survivor who's had this idea? Weapons are the priority. We're going to need ammo to get the medicine, anyway. Unless you think you can fight your way in with just a hatchet."

"I don't feel right stealing," I confessed.

"Seriously? You don't want to break into a house, but your whole plan is to break into a school? What's the difference?"

"It's public property."

"Dude! Get over it. The world's different now," she said, swerving around another creeper in the road. "You can't survive if you won't scavenge. A house is either occupied, infested, or abandoned. If there's no car, they either drove away as fast as they could, or they're dead. It's not like they hopped over to the market for some eggs."

"If they left, they probably took all their weapons and medicine with them," I countered. "If they're home, they're going to attack looters whether they're infected or not."

"You don't know that!" Ellie raised her voice. "What if the cars are gone because they weren't home when it started? Then the house would be fully stocked. If they left in a panic, who knows what they left inside."

"I know you're worried about safety. Once we get to the refugee center, we'll find a creeper cop, and take it out. Or better yet, a dead cop. It'll have a gun. That's the safest plan. It's only a couple miles away. We'll come back when your leg is better."

"Two miles of creepers away."

"I don't think you understand. If we let that infection go, you'll lose your leg. We need a safe place to rest and treat it."

"It's not that bad!" She was raising her voice, jerking the steering wheel more angrily.

"We need medicine right now! The refugee center is our best shot. This argument is stupid!"

Ellie yanked on the emergency brake and brought the mail truck to a skidding stop. "You may think I'm stupid, but I'm the one driving! I'm searching these houses until I find some ammo. Now give me my hatchet." She yanked her hatchet out of my hand and hopped out of the mail truck.

"Ellie, wait!" I yanked the roll door, but it was still stuck. "That's not what I meant!" I pulled the hammer from my belt, wedged the claw under the latch and pulled. It popped open and the roll door shot up.

Ellie stood behind the truck with a horrified look on her face. The creeper was still there. Its hands were crushed and folded back, but its arms and torso were intact, and its head hung under the bumper. The body had dragged on the pavement the entire way. All the flesh and muscle below the sternum was torn away, exposing its ribs and trailing its internal organs along the road. Below the waist was nothing but strings of blood and gristle.

It was still breathing, quietly. I could actually see its lungs inflating through its ribs. It lifted its head and its nose was a triangular cave in its face. Its front teeth and chin were ground flat by the pavement, and it was snapping its back molars together, trying to bite anything it could. The eyes were gone, and its forehead was torn open with bits of brain matter oozing out.

It couldn't see us but it must have heard us, or maybe smelled us, because it reached for me with a mangled hand. I was horrified.

Ellie thwacked the creeper's neck with her hatchet, and the head rolled under the mail truck. The body went limp, and when air left its lungs, black muck bubbled out of its neck.

I puked in a box of voter guides, and looked back at the trail of creeper guts in the road. We had turned around a bend, so I couldn't see them, but I could hear more of them coming, and getting closer.

"**W**e have to move!" I grabbed Ellie's wrist. "Get back in the truck!"

"No way!" She yanked her hand away. "Hide in the bushes. They'll walk right by and we're scot-free. I'm not leading a mob of creepers all the way to a school full of creepers. It's suicide! Now come on." Ellie limped to the stoop of a house and ducked behind a half wall that enclosed the porch.

I turned back and forth between the truck and the house. The rumble of creepers was getting louder, like a chorus of moans, and a drumbeat of foot falls. "Damn it!" I ran to the porch.

They didn't see us, but they went for the mail truck. The first wave smashed up against the back of it and poured around the sides. As more piled on, the truck began to roll.

A creeper slapped its bloody palm on the driver's side window and Stinky perked up in the seat.

"Stin...!" Ellie yanked my shirt collar, choking my words.

"Shut up. You want them to hear you?" she whispered. "There's nothing you can do."

Stinky's eyes widened as they locked with mine. He put his paws on the glass and I watched in terror as the mail truck rolled away, creepers surrounding it.

I ran into the street and watched the mail truck veer, and tumble off the road. I heard snapping branches, crushing metal, and a huge splash as a creepers followed it over the edge.

I ran to the edge of the road and looked down. The truck was at the bottom of a steep embankment, on its side in a fast-flowing creek. The mountain runoff was rushing around the wrecked frame. Water carried packages and envelopes downstream. Some creepers were trapped under the vehicle, while others flailed in the muddy brook. Some were swept away by the current.

"Stinky!" I yelled, but there was no sign of him.

The creepers heard me, and came toward me, if they could, but got stuck in the mud. It would take them a long time to climb back to the road.

Stinky jumped through the broken windshield and stepped out onto the front bumper. *He was alive!*

A creeper pinned under the truck tried to grab him, but Stinky leapt to a low-hanging branch, just out of reach. Stinky climbed through the trees, all the way back to the road, and jumped into my arms. I clutched him close to my body, soaking wet and shivering, and carried him back to the house.

"You realize you almost got Stinky killed?" I was mad. "And I suppose now you want to walk the rest of the way on that foot?" I yelled.

Ellie was standing in the front door, grinning like a jack-o-lantern.

"What the heck are we supposed to do now?"

She pulled car keys off a hook beside the door and jingled them above her head. "Let's find out, shall we?"

Stinky was still damp when we snuck into the house. He squirmed to get out of my arms, so I put him down. He began bathing himself, licking his paws and wiping them over his head.

The house smelled like death. It was dark, except for the living room, which was lit by a bay window in the front. The wall near the foyer was covered in three generations of photographs. Babies, puppies, and family vacations. A smiling couple eating cake under a banner that read, "Congratulations Livia and Andre!" Black and white prom photos. An old man in a black robe was bursting with pride, holding a wooden gavel. He was a judge.

A photo of a boy in an orange jacket caught my eye. He was holding two dead rabbits, and the judge was next to him, holding a bolt action rifle. I needed to find that gun. I tapped the picture frame to get Ellie's attention. She nodded, and we moved into the living room.

Gray dust covered everything. A flat-screen TV hung on the wall over a case of old VHS tapes. A shelf held books on travel and nutrition. There was a globe, and a vintage, olive-green sofa, and commemorative plates of presidents I'd never heard of. It looked more like a museum than a home, like these people had cocooned themselves in memories, instead of actually living. It was the home of grandparents.

I lit my headlamp as I moved into the dark hallway, clutching my hammer with both hands. I tensed and shook as I searched the gloomy house. The unfamiliar surroundings, with creepers possibly around any corner, made my heart race.

"Thump! Thump! Thump!"

Ellie banged her hatchet on the wall.

"What are you doing!? We need to keep quiet!" I protested.

"Why? If people are alive, I want them to know we're not dead. If there are dead inside, I'd rather face them out here, in the light. Worst-case scenario, we go back outside and trap them in here."

"Good point." There *was* a genius to her recklessness! It was time I learned to trust it. "But I wish you wouldn't call them *dead*."

"Why?" she asked. "They are."

She pulled her mom's flashlight out, and kept close to me, our eyes locked on the dark hallway. The house was so silent I could hear my heart beating.

I continued in whispers. "They're still people, just sick. We should just call them *infected*."

Her voice took on a grave tone. "We're all infected."

I did not expect that answer. "How did you find out?"

She paused in the hallway. "I figured it out. It's the only thing that explains why dead people come back even if they never got bit." She looked back at me to gauge my response. She seemed to be hiding something. "How did *you* figure it out?" she asked.

"Dad was a virologist. He figured it out before he died. The creepers carry the active virus in their blood and saliva, but we've all got a hidden virus that's airborne. That's why people behind walls and in safe zones still turn."

"Your dad was studying the virus?" She didn't seem surprised, and turned her attention back to the hallway ahead.

"Yeah."

"And that's why you think there's a cure?"

"Yeah. I have his research. I just need to find someone who can finish what he started."

She considered this very seriously before she went on. "Max, there's no cure, and they're not sick. They die. Their hearts stop, and they come back as those things. Whoever they were before is gone."

"You don't know that!" I yelled.

She pointed her flashlight forward. "The coast looks clear. Let's rock this place." She charged in, hatchet in one hand and flashlight in the other. Her limp didn't slow her down. Stinky rushed into the darkness ahead of us.

I held back and searched the kitchen. There was a loud crunch when I stepped onto the tiles, and I turned my light down. The kitchen cupboards were left open, and the shelves were mostly empty. Whoever emptied them did it in such a hurry that they let dishes shatter all over the floor.

There were various spices, raw flour, and sugar left in the cupboards. On the counter there was a dish of pink Himalayan salt, a flask of flaxseed oil, and three mason jars labeled "local honey," "wild rice," and "pure maple syrup." Most of it was not worth the weight to carry, but it made the place a decent spot to hold out if we got desperate. The fridge had produce: kale, carrots, cucumbers, apples, organic cottage cheese, and raw milk. All spoiled rotten. The bread was like a big, green moldy sponge. There was nothing canned or any dry food worth taking.

"Looks like this place was already hit," I called.

Ellie yelled, "There's meds in the bathroom!"

I grabbed the honey and wild rice, and followed her voice down the hall. She was rummaging through the bathroom cabinets. The room had a tropical theme, with sailboats on the shower curtain and palm trees on the wallpaper. Driftwood hung on the wall above a gold sink basin shaped like a seashell.

Ellie was pouring green capsules into her mouth. As soon as she saw my face, she put down the bottle. "What? It hurts!" Her mouth was full of pills.

"Do you even know what you're taking?" I asked.

"It says *pain reliever*," she answered, "for *anxiety and psychological stress*. I've definitely got that."

It was valerian root. "Did you see where it says to take it for sleep disorders? Valerian is a sedative!"

"Oh." She spit the capsules back in the bottle and pointed to the medicine cabinet. "Check it out. It's full of stuff."

I focused on prescription meds. Blood pressure meds, antidepressants, muscle relaxants. "We'll take it all." I found sleeping pills, allergy pills, and antipsychotics, but no antibiotics.

"What if the infected retain some part of who they were?" I asked, filling my gear bag. "They have memories. I've seen them do simple things, like swing a tennis racket, or try to shave. Maybe it's like amnesia, and they can be taught again. Maybe they can learn who they were before."

She was shaking her head before I even finished. "When I was on the road, I saw them do all kinds of things. It's just muscle memory. That doesn't make them human. They kill people!"

"People kill people, and they're still human!" I exclaimed.

The shower curtain rustled and my blood went cold. She pushed her hatchet into my hand, and I pushed it back, but she insisted. She was right. In her condition, I should do the hacking. I held the hatchet above my head, braced myself and gestured for her to pull the curtain. She grabbed it and I nodded.

She yanked the curtain back. Inside the tub, Stinky was lapping up the stagnant water that had collected in the bottom. He looked up at me, his tail jittering with excitement before he leapt out of the tub and trotted out of the room.

We exhaled in relief. I let the hatchet hang heavy at my side. I was exhausted.

"A creeper doesn't think," Ellie continued. "It doesn't hesitate. It doesn't choose. It just kills. And the people it kills get up and kill. We still have a choice. To fight or run. To live or die. We still have freewill."

I didn't want to accept that, but there was a ring of truth to it. "Maybe you're right."

She smiled. "What did you just say?"

"I said you're right."

"That's what I like to hear." She grabbed the hatchet back and followed Stinky into the next room.

I grinned, cinched my gear bag shut, and followed.

Ellie and Stinky stood in the dining room. The stench was so thick I had to cover my mouth. The urge to puke was almost overwhelming.

Ellie's flashlight fixed on a woman sitting at the table. She was slumped in her chair with her back to us, dressed in a white wedding gown and a veil over her head. Blood had soaked through it and covered her midsection.

I nudged the woman with my hammer, but she didn't move. It looked like there was a head wound, but I didn't have the stomach to lift the shroud. My headlamp lit the grim scene as I moved around the table, which was set with fine dinnerware, the kind people use for weddings and funerals. The plates were white porcelain with gold leaf around the rim. The glasses were clear with the same gold pattern around the lip. The serving dishes, pitcher, tiered dessert stand, and gravy boat matched the porcelain. The utensils and center candelabra matched the gold color.

There was no food; only a drink had been served.

At the far end of the table was a man in a white tuxedo, head flung back, mouth hung wide. In front of him sat a glass half full of clear liquid. I sniffed it cautiously and a noxious smell burned my nostrils. There was a newly opened, but nearly empty bottle of Granite State Vodka. It was a commemorative liquor sold by the state of New Hampshire to fund the repair of dilapidated state flags, except they never managed to make any money at it.

I poured the glass back in the bottle and stuffed it in my bag, knowing that strong alcohol makes a good disinfectant or fire starter.

I nudged the man with my hammer. He was dead, too. From behind, I saw the gunshot through his head.

Between his knees was the rifle in the photo. I grabbed the barrel, but it was caught under the table. I yanked it, pulling up the man's leg and knocking him on his back. Dust choked my headlamp beam. When it settled, I could see his big toe was stuck in the trigger guard. I tried to twist the rifle free, but the rotten toe came free instead. I popped the toe out with a spoon.

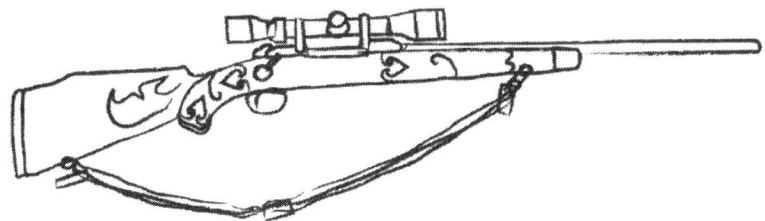

I checked the rifle to make sure it was unloaded, and safe to handle. It was a customized Winchester 70 Featherweight, a classic deer hunting rifle, with a scope, and a fancy, gold-engraved walnut stock. The steel bolt handle, trigger guard, and chamber had similar floral etchings. The ornament was expensive, but it served no purpose beyond show. Along the barrel, in gold calligraphy, it read "Live Free or Die," the increasingly ironic motto of New Hampshire. This thing was more art than artillery.

It was dusty, but well-balanced and in good repair. I found a box of shells in the man's jacket pocket with eight rounds left. I looked back at Ellie, holding the rifle triumphantly, but she was fixed on a frame above the fireplace behind me. Under the gore and brains, behind the bullet-pierced glass, were embroidered letters which read, "God Bless the Burkes."

I couldn't say if Ellie was right about the creepers being alive or dead, but either way surviving in this new world was terrifying. Given the option, this was obviously Judge Burke's choice.

We finished searching the Burke home, but found nothing else of value. A gun safe in the bedroom was empty, which made me think the looters had been family. How else would they know the combination? They probably didn't find the rifle because they couldn't bear to disturb the body.

Ellie found a chainsaw in the garage, but we both agreed it'd be a stupid weapon. It was too noisy and once it was out of gas, it was worthless.

Their car was gone, but I found something way more fun under a tarp in the garage. It was a vintage 1966, gas-powered golf cart by Harvey Davison. It was purple with orange flames that were so bright I felt warmer just looking at them. The name of the machine was written across the rear bumper: *Phaedrus*, which means "radiant" in Greek, but to me it meant "quality."

Phaedrus wasn't just well-maintained; someone loved it. It had two seats, a small pickup bed, and a full tank of gas. I turned the key and the engine roared with the signature rumble of motorcycles from the same brand. It was *perfect*!

"Awesome!" Ellie jumped with giddiness at the sound of it. "Move over! I want to drive."

I planted my hands on the wheel and gave her the most serious look I could muster. "I'm going to have to ask to see your driver's license."

She looked at me in disbelief, then we both erupted in laughter. I scooted over to let her take the wheel and called for Stinky. He came running and jumped into my lap. It was stupid to rev the engine. The sound would attract every creeper in earshot, but it was irresistible. We tied our gear down, rolled to the end of the driveway, and Ellie pressed the gas to the floor as we flew down the hill, back on track.

Phaedrus didn't have a speedometer, but the wind gave my face such a chill it felt like the fastest I had ever gone. When we hit bumps in the road, the little speeder caught air, which made my stomach drop. I clutched Stinky close and grabbed the dashboard, afraid we might fly out, but Ellie rode the jumps with exhilaration, turning rapidly around abandoned cars and other debris. I was terrified, but didn't want to ruin her fun, or waste any time.

We came to a T-intersection at the bottom of the hill. Highway 75 was a big name for what was actually just a small two-lane road. Ellie spun Phaedrus to a halt, spinning in a half circle with the nose pointed back up the hill.

"Whooh! That was so sick!" She pumped her fist in the air.

"Sure was." I faked a laugh and tried to hide the fact that I might actually be sick.

She clutched her chest before slumping back into the seat, heaving for air.

"Are you okay?"

She nodded. "Yeah, just a little dizzy."

"Let me drive the rest of the way. It's all flat from here, anyway." She agreed and we switched places, Stinky switching laps.

I headed south at a comfortable speed to keep the engine quiet.

"What gives? Why'd you slow down?"

I pointed to our right as we passed the Pine Grove Cemetery. I used to walk by it on my way to school. Mom was buried there.

Ellie looked, and turned to me, wiggling her outstretched fingers, "They're coming to get you."

"Not funny."

She continued in a goofy voice, "Look! Here comes one now."

"Stop acting like a child!"

"News flash, Brainiac. I *am* a child." She slumped back in her seat. "And so are you."

We rolled past the graveyard in silence. I wasn't worried about ghouls digging out of their graves, like in the movies. The physics of it was absurd. They'd grind their fingers to the knuckle before they even got through the coffin. Still, the thought of some corpse clawing against the dark forever made me feel claustrophobic.

I briefly wondered if digging them up, and comparing the burial dates of graves that had reanimated corpses, might give us the exact time of the airborne virus' outbreak. But there was no time. Ellie needed medicine.

After we passed the cemetery Ellie said, "Don't be so serious. We've got food. We've got bullets. We've got wheels. Life is good."

I half-smiled and revved the engine. What we didn't have was time, but I didn't say anything.

We passed the Sugar Plum Golf Course where Judge Burke must have showed off Phaedrus. It had a gift shop and a gas station. I made a mental note to go back if we ever needed engine parts and gas.

Just south of the golf course, we crossed a bridge over the creek. We were at least two miles downstream, and junk mail was still floating by. What if the creepers had contaminated the water, maybe even the fish?

The creek divided rural Thornton from downtown, although all of Thornton was pretty rural. We started passing political campaign signs along the side of the road. "Governor Mark Warden: Less Government = More Liberty" and "America's Toughest Sheriff: Bradley Napolitano." There were national election signs too, but they weren't worth much more than kindling anymore, if they ever were. The Capitol may as well have been another planet.

Many larger properties in that area had pastures for raising animals, mostly horses, but the creepers had already gotten any beast that was fenced in. Half-eaten livestock were lying in the fields.

I didn't see any creepers on the road. In fact, there were no signs of life at all. Maybe everyone evacuated early. Maybe the creepers had wandered down the road... but then, wouldn't the creepers up the road have wandered here?

There were abandoned vehicles everywhere; even some RVs. Homes in this area had piles of chopped firewood stacked and ready for winter heating. Building supplies were stacked around various homes still under construction. The large brick houses looked as secure as castles. Many had private wells that wouldn't be contaminated by the creek. Roadside stands were stocked with homemade maple syrup and fruit preserves. It was technically illegal, but lots of families with fruit trees or sugar maples ran stands for extra money.

The world looked so empty it was spooky, but it looked like there was an endless supply of resources, even though they would be dangerous to salvage. I knew we were near the refugee center when I saw signs to reduce speed in a school zone. I did the opposite.

Phaedrus rolled to a halt as we approached the school. The campus was a militarized zone.

The street was blocked with police barricades, but we easily walked through the openings between them. Inside, Thornton Police armored vehicles and cruisers formed a visual perimeter, but it looked like no one had kept watch for some time.

The road in front of the campus was littered with corpses, some gunned down, others eaten up. It must have been a horrific battle.

Ellie had fallen asleep along the final stretch. She was exhausted. I was exhausted, too.

"Ellie," I nudged her gently. "Wake up!" I patted her burning-hot cheeks. Her eyes circled wildly in her head as she tried to get a lock on me. "Ellie, it's time to move."

She looked delirious. "No good. I'll just slow you down. Leave me here."

"No way! You're totally exposed here. Besides, I need you." I pointed toward the closest armored vehicle. The Ballistic Engineered Armored Response Counter Attack Truck, or BEARCAT, was a wheeled personnel carrier designed for the military, but the Thornton Police Department got two by partnering with the Joint Terrorism Task Force.

23

They called them "rescue vehicles" when they got them, but the gun ports, roof hatches, and battering rams seemed like overkill to most people at the time. "You'll be safer in that thing, and you can keep a lookout."

Ellie nodded, but she was looking weak. I helped her up to the top of the BEARCAT, passed her Stinky and all our gear, strapped the rifle to my back, and climbed up. From the top, I could see the lay of the land.

The school was a set of boxy, gray buildings connected by a breezeway, much like a prison. The flag flew at half-mast and all the windows were boarded up. The largest building was two floors high and housed the auditorium, faculty lounge, and some classrooms. The main building housed the administrative offices, the cafeteria, and more classrooms. A helicopter was perched on the roof of the main office.

The front of the campus was enclosed in a head-high black fence with thick vertical black bars, and cross bars at the top and bottom for support. Every twenty yards or so, the fence was mounted to red brick columns. There were gates at both ends of the driveway, and a third gate on the south side of the campus leading to the senior faculty parking lot.

The main lot was filled with civilian cars, emergency vehicles, and a school bus parked in the passenger loading zone near the front entrance.

The soccer field on the north side of the campus was filled with olive-green refugee tents and mobile units. Parked between the tents and the parking lot were two ambulances and a Health Department mobile command vehicle.

Beyond the main parking lot, alongside the main building, was a smaller tent cluster enclosed by its own internal chain-link fence. It looked like an improvised police headquarters, and in the center was a large, white tent with a huge red cross on its roof. *A medical tent!*

The only problem was the dozens of creepers between me and the tent. The upside was there was no herd; the creepers were all spread out. At first glance, the refugee center looked like it was bustling with survivors, except there were no signs of actual life, just wandering gray bodies. No direction. No leader. It had been a while since they had anything to chase. Luckily, they were penned in by the fences.

I pointed out the medical tent to Ellie. "That's where I'm headed first. If there are antibiotics left, that's where they'd be." I dumped out the main pouch of my gear bag. "I'm leaving everything with you. I'll need the space."

"How're you going to get there? It's a dead zone."

I sifted through the pile of stuff and grabbed a bottle of Free Breeze.

"Air freshener?" she asked skeptically.

"I tested it at Lochshire. They track by smell. If they can't smell me, and I act like them, they'll ignore me." I pushed the bottle into my belt. "I'm taking a radio. You'll be my eyes up here."

She nodded, half-convinced. "You need to keep quiet, or they'll come after you. Take these." She pulled a zPod out of her front pocket, and unwound the ear buds. "Plug these in your radio so they can't hear me."

"Good thinking. Thanks."

"Take this." She handed me her hatchet. "I'll take the rifle and cover you. That way, the gunfire will draw them in my direction, not yours."

Rifles are better as long-range weapons, and we didn't have many options. I handed it to her and started showing her how to load it, but she took it from me and did it herself, already familiar with firearms.

She crouched into a firing stance and shrieked in pain. Her leg was getting worse.

"Let me check that before I go." She turned so I could see her ankle. I unwrapped the bandage and peeled the gauze back, which was wet with pus and blood. The wound had an awful, sour smell, a sign of serious infection. My stitches still held the wound closed, but it wasn't healing. It was turning black, and her calf was swollen and warm to the touch. Red streaking showed the infection was spreading in her bloodstream. I began feeling her upper leg for more swelling.

"Whoa! You flirting with me or what?" she joked.

"What? No, I'm just... " I blushed. "See here?" I pressed lightly on her inner thigh and she winced. "Your lymph nodes are swollen. It's like a sore throat when the lymph nodes in your neck swell up. It means your immune system is fighting the infection."

"That's good, right?"

No, it wasn't good. This was a full-blown medical emergency. "You're gonna be fine," I said, trying not to panic her. "I'm gonna go get the antibiotics, and you're gonna be fine."

I opened my trauma kit, grabbed new sterile gauze, and wet it with the vodka from Judge Burke's house. "This is going to sting." I covered the wound with the pad. She cried out and quickly covered her mouth. She pounded against the hatch of the BEARCAT with muffled screams, her eyes tearing up. I rewrapped her ankle, keeping the bandage smooth, but not too tight. "It's almost over," I said. "We're going to get through this."

She nodded and grabbed my hand. "Max?"

"Yeah?"

"If I get through this, I want to come with you to your cabin. If that's okay with you."

No one had ever called Dad's cabin mine before. But she was right, it was mine. Now that he was gone, it was safe to say I had inherited it, though I would never stop thinking of it as Dad's cabin. At least, not yet. I was still adjusting to the reality that he was gone. "Of course. PorcScouts Rule #27. *No one is an island.*"

"What's Pork Scouts?"

"It's *Porc*, as in Porcupine Freedom Scouts. It's like a club, about teaching survival skills, building good character, and learning mental self-defense, like learning how to think logically."

"That's where you learned this medical stuff?"

"Yeah, and why I'm going to the cabin. The other PorcScout families might be there if they're still alive."

"Why porcupines?"

I'd never asked that question, never even considered it, but decided the answer must be, "Because they're lethal, but only in self-defense." I helped her back into a firing posture.

"Max," her voice was breathy and weak. I could tell there was a lot that she wanted to say, but all that came out was, "Don't get bit."

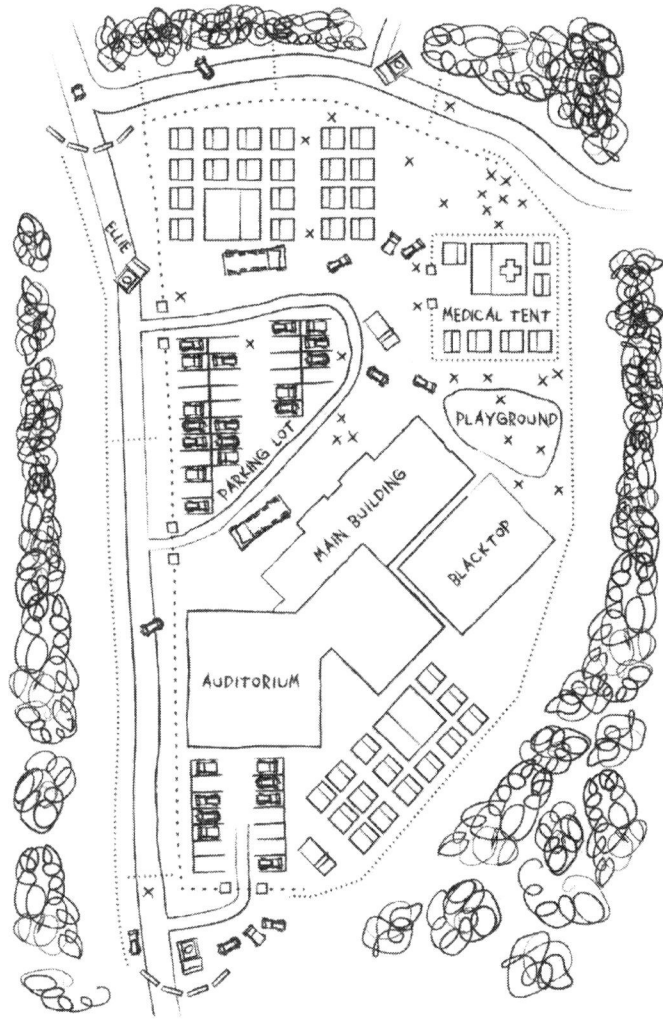

Stinky was determined to follow me as I climbed out of the BEARCAT. "No, Stinky." I picked him up and put him back in the BEARCAT. "You have to stay with Ellie." He started to jump out, but I put my hand out to block him. "No. Don't worry. I'll be right back." He circled, meowed, and settled next to Ellie's leg.

I hopped out with the hatchet in one hand and Dad's radio in the other. I pushed the button and brought it to my face. "Check, check."

"I'm here." Ellie's weak voice came back over the radio.

"Stay with me," I said, adjusting the ear buds so I could hear her more clearly. I looked up and saw her head poking out of the BEARCAT, watching me through the rifle scope. "I need you to walk me through." She had a better view of the area, and I wanted to keep her conscious.

"How are you getting in?" she asked.

"Look over there," I said as I pointed to a dead cop dressed in riot gear. "That's my way in."

The cop was dressed in all black with armored plates on its arms and legs, a helmet with a face shield, and a Kevlar vest with "POLICE" in white letters. I nicknamed it *Officer Friendly*.

"Max, that hatchet is no good against that thing. That helmet will stop a bullet."

"I'm not gonna kill it." I ran up to the wrought iron fence and hid behind a brick column next to the driveway. I peeked around and spotted Officer Friendly a few feet away. It stood with its back to me, as if it was guarding the gate. Was it waiting for refugees? Or was it just muscle memory?

I didn't see any creepers on my side of the fence. "How many in the front lot?" I whispered into the radio.

"Five," she answered. "Only one has a clear path. The rest are behind cars."

"Watch this." I took a deep breath and tapped the blade of the hatchet against the metal bracket, where the fence connected to the column.

"Ting! Ting! Ting!"

Officer Friendly gave a curious grunt that told me I had its attention. I banged the fence with a *"clang!"*

The riot cop shoved its arms through the fence and reached around the brick column I was hiding behind, trying to snatch whatever was making the sound. I ducked, and its grasping fingers met above my head. I inched sideways and grabbed a bundle of plastic zip ties hanging off its belt. Cops use them as restraints when they make mass arrests.

I cinched its wrists together on my side of the fence. Neutralized!

"Ha! Did you see that?" I exclaimed into the radio.

"See if it has a gun. And keep your voice down."

"Right!" I reached for Officer Friendly's pockets through the fence, groping its sides. I never thought I'd be frisking a cop. I accidentally plunged my hand into an open wound on its side. Something had taken a big bite out of it. I wiped the blood on its pants.

Officer Friendly yanked on its restraint, but couldn't get free. It pressed its face against the bars, but its helmet was too big. It roared, jerking back and forth, and then it stopped struggling. It just watched me. I hadn't seen a creeper behave this way before.

My heart pounded as its stare burned into me. I didn't see unthinking hunger. Its rage seemed almost human. It was analyzing me.

"Incoming!" warned Ellie.

I peeked over its shoulder. A woman in a bloody hospital gown was headed my way, attracted to the noise.

I felt a bulge in Officer Friendly's vest pouch. I opened it and found a Sig Sauer Mosquito. It was small, but better than nothing. It was probably his backup weapon.

The woman crashed into the fence, and I backed up, tucking the pistol in the back of my pants. I had eight zip ties and easily cinched the woman's wrists too. Behind it, more creepers trickled out of refugee tents toward the commotion.

I moved along the fence, spacing them out and restraining them as they lunged through the bars.

"Ting! Ting! Ting!"

Zip!

"Ting! Ting! Ting!"

Zip!

When I ran out of zip ties, I started poking them with the hatchet to rile them up. That way, the stragglers would go for them instead of me. The seven civilians clamored against the fence, howling like animals, but not Officer Friendly. It was different, like the Postman. Not calm, but tense. Tilting its head and watching me.

I gulped when I saw Officer Friendly grinding the zip tie against the edge of the brick column. It was trying to escape. It understood!

I ran to the other driveway and hid behind another column. The gate was unlocked, and I inched it open.

"Keep low," came Ellie's voice. "You can sneak between the cars most of the way to the medical tent."

"I have a better idea." I sprayed myself with the air freshener until the nozzle sputtered out. I shook the can and tried again, but it was gone.

"Make it count," she cautioned.

I looked back at the BEARCAT, surprised she could see from so far away. She had a good view through the scope. I nodded, held my finger to my lips to shush her, and attached the radio to my belt. I slipped through the gate, put my head down, hung my arms low with both hands clutching the hatchet, and shambled toward the medical tent.

Creepers lurked toward Officer Friendly and the others. As I approached the school, I noticed that its steel doors were peppered with bullet holes. The school bus was full of students, sitting in rows, wasting away. Bloody handprints on the windows told the story.

Past the main building, I saw the field behind the campus, where dozens more creepers were lurking around.

Three creepers came around the corner and my stomach turned when I recognized the leader. It was Officer Pike, the school resource officer. It was fresher than the others and had no visible injuries. It didn't look *that* dead, except for the pinhole eyes and the gray face. Its jerky step and slack neck were a dead giveaway.

I glanced around, seeing all the familiar faces for the first time. I saw my old teachers and classmates. The clerk from the general store, my old barber, and the Thornton librarian were all there. This wasn't a compound of the undead. It was an open graveyard of all my friends and neighbors.

As Officer Pike and its pack went by, I tightened my grip on the hatchet to keep my hands from shaking. I gave them a sideways glance as we shuffled by each other. The air freshener was working!

I held my breath as the last one turned toward me. Its nose whistled and gurgled as it took deep, slow breaths. I braced myself to swing, but it lost interest and I kept moving toward the medical tent.

The entrance gate to the police tents was torn off its hinges and lying flat. Riot cops stood on both sides. One was holding a shotgun, but it was too risky to take. The other was disarmed, literally. It was missing an arm. They were slouched and awkward looking, but they looked like they were guarding the entrance, just like Officer Friendly. Was this really just muscle memory?

As I inched passed them, they looked me over, but didn't leave their posts. Relief surged through my body as I found the medical tent. Once inside, I closed the entrance flap with Velcro latches.

Three bodies were laid out on steel tables and covered in sheets. *Creepy!*

"I'm in!" I whispered into the radio.

"I can't believe that worked. Hurry! This party you started is about to rip the fence down."

"Did they see you?"

"I don't think so."

"Hang tight, I'm almost done."

I rummaged around and found a tub labeled "Antibiotics" in a steel refrigerator. There were a dozen bottles of clear liquids, with names like Amoxicillin and Cephazolin. "I found them, but I don't know what these names mean."

"Grab anything labeled 'broad-spectrum.'"

"I hope you're not afraid of needles."

"If we're using an IV, make sure and grab extra saline solution," she instructed.

"How do you know that?"

"Let's just say this ain't my first rodeo."

I put all the bottles in my gear bag. Better safe than sorry. I also took a handful of prefilled saline syringes.

On the wall, I spotted a poster that showed step-by-step instructions for administering an IV. I grabbed some alcohol swabs, and any tubes or clamps that looked like what was shown in the pictures. On my way out, I ripped down the poster, and threw my gear bag over my shoulder.

"Got it! I'm coming back!"

I pushed the tent flap aside and stepped into the cool air.

Ellie's voice interrupted. "Max, you have company!"

It was Officer Friendly, and its hands were scraped and bloody from grinding against the bricks. Its eyes locked with mine, showing something more than hunger or rage. It was recognition. Somehow, this had become personal.

Officer Friendly came running at me in a full sprint, and I froze, never having seen an infected move so fast. I was paralyzed and my body went cold with fear.

A gunshot echoed across the campus as Officer Friendly's helmet burst, sending glass and brains flying. In the distance, Ellie screamed.

The pain was quick and hot. I looked at the blood on my hand, and before I realized it was mine, I was on the ground. The bullet had passed through Officer Friendly's head and struck my right shoulder, below my collarbone.

Ellie was frantic on the radio, but I couldn't follow what she was saying. Everything started feeling hazy. The blood pooling under me was warm, but I still felt cold.

Chapter Eight: Only Eight Rounds

My head whirled until I was so dizzy I thought the world might slip away. Between my deafening heart beats, I heard a muffled rumbling. The ground shook and pulled me back to consciousness.

It got louder, and closer, until it was not a single hum, but distinct overlapping thumps all blending together. I barely heard the second gunshot over the clamor, but then I knew what the sound was. The herd was awake.

A third shot. *She'd run out soon.* The thought came to me in my stupor. With each shot, the footfalls quickened. They were headed toward Ellie.

I sat up, my shoulder burned like fire. The hatchet rested in a pool of my blood. I grabbed it with my good arm.

A fourth shot.

I pushed myself up with the hatchet handle to get to my feet. I felt delirious, like I might pass out from blood loss. My wound gushed as I staggered toward the entrance.

A fifth shot.

I stumbled over the fallen gate and braced myself against the perimeter fence. The herd came pouring out of the refugee tents and the field behind the main building. They came out of bushes, cars, and other hiding places. If they couldn't run, they walked. If they couldn't walk, they crawled. They acted in unison, like a single organism, pursuing relentlessly to see if the sound was friend or food.

A sixth shot.

The herd piled against the outer fence. I yelled into the radio, but Ellie didn't answer. The fence held, but there was no telling for how long. The creepers climbed on top of each other to get over the fence and I could see Ellie taking aim at one that reached the other side.

A seventh shot.

Two riot cops heard me yelling and turned toward me. I tightened my grip on the hatchet as they approached.

The eighth and final shot rang out. Ellie was out of ammo.

I lifted the hatchet with my good arm and swung for the first cop's face. It slid off the helmet and embedded in the shoulder plate. Blood spurted as the riot cop screamed in pain, falling to one knee.

Creepers don't scream in pain, I thought.

The second cop pulled my arms behind my back. The twinge of the bracelets tightening was nothing compared to the pain in my shoulder, but all I felt was relief.

Creepers don't take prisoners.

Ellie screamed over the roar of the crowd.

My captor forced me to the ground with his knee in my back. Two more riot cops flew overhead. I thought I was hallucinating, but they were on a zip line from the roof of the school to the street. I hadn't noticed it before because it looked like a phone line.

These were survivors. This was their rescue team.

I went limp with my face in the dirt. The cop with the injured shoulder barked with a clenched jaw, "Stop resisting." His baton came down hard on my skull, and the world slipped away.

I could make out hushed voices in the room, but everything was a blur. I felt disoriented. My eyes were closed, but fluorescent light burned through my eyelids. I tried to sit up, but couldn't. I was paralyzed.

"Max Hartwell?" The voice was a whisper, but familiar. It was Mrs. Mills, the school nurse. She sounded concerned, and skeptical. She probably thought I was dead.

"The homeschool kid?" The snarky voice was Miss Styx, the school guidance counselor.

I was shirtless on a table. The cold steel made me shiver.

"Poor things. Out there alone, all this time," said Nurse Mills.

A male voice interrupted, stern but still hushed. "That 'poor thing' just about took my arm off, and the other one just killed Markus." I didn't recognize his voice.

"You big baby," mocked Nurse Mills. "It's just a scratch. I'll patch you up when I'm done here, and you know Markus wasn't exactly alive, anyway."

The man scoffed.

Nurse Mills continued. "After that, I'll give you your inspection."

"Why? I didn't even make contact!"

"Doesn't matter. That's the rules. Everyone gets searched for bites and scratches every time they go out. Even you. You know this."

My arms were at my sides. I tried to wiggle my toes, but they were too numb to tell if it was working.

"Who's the girl?" asked Miss Styx in a suspicious tone.

"I don't know," Mrs. Mills sighed. "She was in septic shock when they brought her in. I put her on a battery of antibiotics and fluid replacement. If her blood pressure doesn't stabilize, we'll use vasopressors, but she's still unconscious."

"Waste of good meds, if you ask me," said the man under his breath.

"Matt!" protested the nurse. "She's just a girl."

"Basic triage, Doc. This is no time to get sentimental. Medicine is gold. If it's not a sure thing, you oughta pull the plug. The boy, too. That bullet went through Markus' head. If he's infected, you're wasting your time."

My heart sped up. Was I infected?

"It's possible the bullet was hot enough to burn off the virus. We have to try," rebutted Nurse Mills. "Besides, they brought in more medicine than we'll use treating them."

"I'm going to remind you about this next time you start complaining that my team isn't bringing home enough supplies." Part of me was glad that I hit Matt with the hatchet.

Feeling was beginning to coming back into my body with a warm sensation, and a tingling in my fingers and toes. Nurse Mills was treating my shoulder.

"They had a lot of food. I'll take it to the faculty lounge for equitable redistribution," announced Miss Styx.

"I'm taking the rifle," insisted Matt. "My team needs all the firepower we can get."

The warm sensation gradually became an intense pain. Nurse Mills was digging around in my shoulder with some kind of utensils. I tried to scream, but I couldn't. I tried to move, but I couldn't. I was chemically paralyzed.

"What about the folder?" asked Nurse Mills. "It looks like some kind of research."

"Talk to Ms. Lessard if you want a copy. It's not my call," Miss Styx said. "Is he waking up?"

"Damn!" Mrs. Mills broke her whisper. "Turn up the drip. We need to keep him under until I get all the bullet fragments out."

I heard them fumbling with equipment, and then everything began to blur again. Before I was gone, I heard Matt say, "Nurse! Look at her leg."

"I know. Hopefully we caught it in time." replied Mrs. Mills.

"No, her other leg. Is that what I think it is?"

"Oh my god!" she exclaimed. "But that's impossible."

And the pain was gone.

I woke up to the electronic "ping" of the school bell. I never thought I'd hear that again.

I found myself on a cot under a thin wool blanket. I sat up and my shoulder ached, but the searing heat was gone. I was shirtless and my chest and arm were crossed with bandages, holding an antiseptic pad over the bullet hole. There was no exit wound.

All my gear was gone.

I was in a small room with tile floors and a fluorescent light. It was a storage closet, but with empty shelves. The door was green with a glass window covered by a poster on the other side. I couldn't see out, but the poster was turned around so I could read it from the inside. It was a drawing of a sinking boat with the caption, "Loose lips sink ships."

I caught my reflection in the glass. My hair was about an inch longer than I remembered it being, and it was starting to hang over my eyes. It had been a while since I'd looked into a mirror. I was thinner than I had been, but I looked wiry. My body was bruised, but hardened, with muscles in places I didn't even know I had them. I almost didn't recognize myself, but this was the new me. The post-collapse me.

Tack. Tack. Tack.

There was a light tapping on the glass, and a man in a police uniform pulled up the poster on the other side. Using only his eyebrows and a head nod, he told me to sit back on the cot, and I complied.

His keys jingled as he unlocked the door and came in, half smiling. I went to shake his hand but he stepped back, and put a hand on his sidearm. "No, you sit right there and don't move." It was Matt. I recognized his voice, which was still practically a whisper. I sat back down. "Good. Now, I'm going to have to ask you some questions."

"Sorry about your arm. I thought you were one of them."

He looked annoyed. "Yeah, well, I'm made of sterner stuff than some deadhead."

"Where's my friend? Can I see her?"

"I don't think so. We're cautious about infection around here, especially since you're from the outside. We're going to keep you here, and hold her for observation. Make sure you're both... healthy."

"What about my cat?"

"What cat?"

"Stinky. He was with my friend."

"No one reported seeing a cat." He scoffed.

"He was there. You have to go get him!" I demanded.

"Hey! Keep your voice down. Sorry to point out the obvious, but rescuing house pets isn't exactly worth risking the lives of my men."

"Fine. Give me my gear. I'll go get him myself." I stood up.

"Sit down!" His voice hit a normal volume, which sounded like barking by comparison. "You're under quarantine. Did you miss the memo? You're not leaving this room."

"You got no right to hold me here!" I met his increased volume.

"We got plenty of right! We got you on assaulting a law enforcement officer, minor in possession of alcohol, not to mention stealing medical supplies."

"You're joking."

"I'm dead serious. We also got your friend on possession of a firearm in a gun-free zone. It's a gray area, but we could probably even trump up a murder charge for that cop she killed. Charge you as an accomplice. Let a jury decide. Of course, it might be a while before we can put a jury together, but you could sit right here until then. You want me to keep going?"

"Do you have any idea what's going on out there?" I protested.

"I know exactly what's going on out there. I'm out there every day with my team, keeping these people safe, keeping them warm and fed. And you know what the key to that is? Keeping those deadheads calm. Now you two punks have jeopardized all that. It'll be days before we get them back on a fixed schedule."

I suddenly remembered the Mosquito tucked in my pants. I felt the hard handle pressed against my tail bone. It had slipped down into my underwear. They must have missed it.

Matt was smug. "Look. I think we got off on the wrong foot. We're just going to keep you here till the Doc says it's safe to let you back into general population. If you cooperate and answer my questions, we're not going to hold you on those charges."

I scowled. "If you want to play by the old rules, then read me my Miranda rights, because I'm not answering any more questions until you get me an attorney. How long do you think that will take?"

Matt laughed. "Food in his belly, medicine in his veins, and now he wants an attorney. If that's how you want to play it, I'll wait. Enjoy your stay, Max. You're going to be in here a long time." He left and locked the door behind him.

I sighed in relief and pulled out the Mosquito. I sat on the cot and checked the cartridge, counting 10 .22LR rounds. I searched for a place to hide it, but the room was barren.

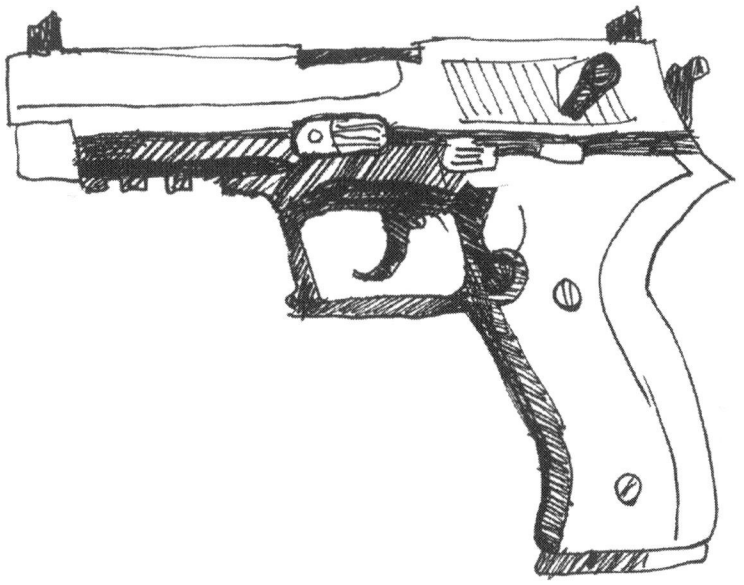

I tucked it under the pillow and flopped down on the cot. For the first time in weeks, I actually relaxed. There were walls, and people with guns defending them. I was safe. Suddenly, my whole body ached with old bruises, but it didn't matter for long because I fell right back to sleep.

*R*ows of white windmills punctuated the coastline against a blue sky. I was with three companions. One I could tell was Ellie, but I didn't recognize the two boys. We were digging in the sand with shovels. Thirteen bodies laid in rows, wrapped in white wool and red tape. Huge, gray waves crashed on the shore, and the wind was just as violent, but warm for the season.

As I tossed ash into the surf, my feet sank to my ankles. I felt something with my toes and dropped the shovel. I scratched at the ground with my hands and discovered a cache of strange trinkets. A yoyo. A calculator. A baseball. A permanent marker. Someone had buried all the property teachers had ever seized from students. There were hundreds of items.

The windmills slowed to a halt, and the ocean went calm. Ellie and the two boys stopped digging and rested on their shovels, watching me.

In the mix of knickknacks, I discovered a pistol, with one end of a long, crimson ribbon tied to the trigger. I pulled on the cord to find the other end and it cut a line in the sand toward the water. It pulled tight on something beneath the waves, and when I yanked it, a casket of a similar color floated to the surface. I was dumbfounded when the soggy crimson coffin creaked open, and a familiar figure emerged.

Dad.

I turned to run, but the thirteen bodies sat up attentively, shoulder-to-shoulder, like a jury judging me through their wool-covered eyes.

Dad yanked the ribbon and the pistol went off in my hand. The bullet found its home in Ellie's heart, and her expression turned from surprise, to pain, and then went slack. When I screamed, the bullet left her body dead, and returned to the gun.

* * *

I bolted awake, screaming with the loaded Mosquito pointed at the door.

There was a knock, and a woman's voice. "Max? You okay?"

I caught my breath and came to my senses, shaking my head. "I'm fine, just… I'm fine." I couldn't say how long I'd been asleep, or what time of day it was. My body shook.

"Can I come in? It's Nurse Mills."

I wiped sweat off my face, and shoved the pistol under the pillow. "Uh, sure."

She cracked the door open, peered in, and then came in. "I'm sorry about Matt. Don't worry, he's not in charge. He's just under a lot of pressure. He means well. I hope you're not upset."

My eyes shifted to a plate of food in her hand.

"I brought you some supper." She put it on a shelf with an apple juice box. "It's not much."

It was a heap of steaming peas and corn, a wedge of mystery meat, and a slice of bread with jam. It didn't matter what was on the plate. I didn't waste a second before I started devouring the meal.

"Thank you," I mumbled through a mouthful of pea mush.

"I wish we had more for you," she said. "You must be ravenous."

I nodded, swirling the bread over the plate to soak up every drip of meat juice.

"I'm here to check on your wounds," she smiled. "And I'll need to inspect you for bites."

"I wasn't bit," I said. "I'd have turned by now if I was."

"If you feel ready, we have a General Assembly every Sunday. This week should be very exciting. We've been preparing for first snow for weeks. You can join us you like."

My mind clamored with questions, but just one word fell out.

"Ellie?"

"Is that your friend? No one recognized her, and she didn't have any ID. We've been calling her Hope."

Hope? "Can I see her?"

"No, I'm sorry." She twirled her hair in her fingers. "Her injuries were more severe, and she's still unconscious. This wouldn't be the right time. But we have a lot of questions about her, about both of you, if you're feeling up to it."

"Am I a prisoner here?"

"Well, no. Not really. Let's see how you feel at the end of the week. Then we'll find you a more comfortable room and show you what we're creating here."

Chapter Twelve: Secret Whispers

I needed a better hiding place for the pistol. PorcScouts Rule #46: *Keep your things in a safe place where no one else looks.* There weren't many options. Above me was a drop ceiling; white panels in a suspended metal grid. I climbed to the top of a shelf, careful not to put weight on my injured arm, pushed a panel up and peered in. There was a crawl space, full of wiring and ventilation ducts. I was small enough that I could escape through the vents, but not until my injuries healed. The grate was fastened with hex screws. I'd need a hex wrench, or a crowbar to open it.

A voice came from deep in the vent. "Hello? Who's there?" It was a girl, barely louder than a whisper.

"Are you talking to me?" I answered.

"Duh, who else? You must be one thousand one hundred and two."

"What?"

"Your refugee number. Everything is counted here. I'm one hundred seventy-two."

"There are over a thousand survivors here?" I was stunned.

"Well, no. That's the people we've counted, not the people who survived," she explained. "Seventy-three people live here now, and when Livia gives birth, that will make seventy-four."

"What's your name?"

"Staci. Who are you?"

I knew her. Well, I knew *of* her. She was a cheerleader or something, one of the popular kids. "I'm Max."

"You're the kid who won the egg drop last year. That was cool," she buzzed.

"That's me. It was just a matter of dispersing the potential energy of the egg before..."

"Whatever, Egghead. Kids are saying your dad invented the walker virus. Is that true?"

"No! What? He was working on a cure!"

"I heard you got bit, but you survived because you bit the walker back. Is that true?"

"No, that's stupid. No one survives a bite," I countered.

"So, how did you survive out there all this time, with no adult supervision?"

"I exploited their weaknesses," I answered.

"What's that supposed to mean?"

"You play your strengths against their weaknesses. Walkers are dumb. That makes them predictable."

"Oh, I get it. Is it true that there are smart walkers?" she asked.

"What's a smart walker?"

"I heard some of them hunt in packs, like wolves, or they make the baby ones cry to trick people. I don't know, but I hear rumors. I've never seen one."

"I've never seen anything like that, either. Some are not as stupid as the others, but I don't think that makes them smart," I explained.

"So, do you think they're getting smarter?"

I pondered that for a moment in silence.

"Are you still there?" she asked.

"Yes. No. No, I don't think they're getting smarter. I think they're different because we're different. I think something about who they were before affects what they become."

"Weird."

"So, where am I?" I asked.

"Well, I'm in the principal's office, so I guess you're in the art room. They always separate new people for about a week to make sure they're not infected."

The art room had a supply closet. I must have been in there. "Why are you in the principal's office?"

"Oh, it's not the principal's office anymore. Principal Bowness is... outside. The Watchers use the main office as the Armory now. I have ammunition duty, so I load magazines and make sure no one takes anything without permission."

"What are Watchers?"

"You don't know anything, do you? There's Watchers and Runners. Watchers keep watch on the roof. Runners go to the town and bring back supplies. They're mostly police, but there are lots of volunteers now. Plus two army guys. They're in charge. Did you hit Officer Cordell with an ax?"

"Yeah. I thought he was a creep... uh... a walker."

She laughed. "You got that right! That guy is a creep. He totally deserved it."

"Is Ellie okay?"

"The girl? I don't know. The faculty won't talk about her." I could hear more voices come into the room. "The Major is here. I gotta go," she whispered. "Whatever you do, keep your voice down. The walkers don't know we're in here. We'll talk more next time I have duty here."

I hid the pistol in the ceiling, and fit the panel back into place. The conversation had my mind spinning.

Chapter Thirteen: Routine

The days blended together, and as time passed, my body mended. At night, the school furnace would kick on. The bell schedule continued, almost like a regular school day. Instead of six one-hour periods with a forty-five minute lunch after fourth period, there were three two-hour periods with a one-hour lunch break after the second period, plus a five-minute break between each period, and a final bell as a thirty minute warning before lights out. It was baffling. *Why didn't the bells draw the creepers in the yard?*

Every day, an officer brought me breakfast, lunch, and dinner. During lunch, I was allowed into the next room—the art room—and given forty-five minutes of supervised exercise.

They made me do twenty neck rolls, twenty jumping jacks, twenty arm circles, and twenty toe touches. It was ridiculous. I had free time after the exercises. They gave me a soccer ball to play with, but I spent my time reading newspapers I found in the trash. They were all from the early days of the outbreak. They must have either stopped delivering, or stopped publishing after the collapse. Headlines like, "Mass Murder Epidemic" and "The Dead Walk" were promising, but the articles didn't say anything I didn't already know. The military said to sever the head or destroy the brain. The Capitol had a double-secret meeting with all the well-armed departments, but never announced any decisions. There were reports of creeper attacks as far as Phoenix. That was a month ago. The outbreak was probably global by now.

Twice, the supervising officer was Sheriff Bradley Napolitano. People called him Sheriff Nap. I recognized him from his campaign signs. He was a permanent institution in Grafton County. Sheriffs were elected every four years, but he never had any serious opposition. People loved him because he left them alone.

The other officers ignored me or told me to keep it down, but Sheriff Nap would hang out and get to know me. He was an Oath Keeper, meaning he took his oath to "defend the Constitution against all enemies, foreign and domestic" more seriously than most cops. In fact, he told me he considered his oath to be to the New Hampshire Constitution, not the Federal Constitution, which meant defending Grafton County from federal enemies. Sheriff Nap was a Granite Stater first, and an American second.

Midweek, they brought me to the locker room to shower and change. It was timed so I wouldn't pass any other refugees in the hall.

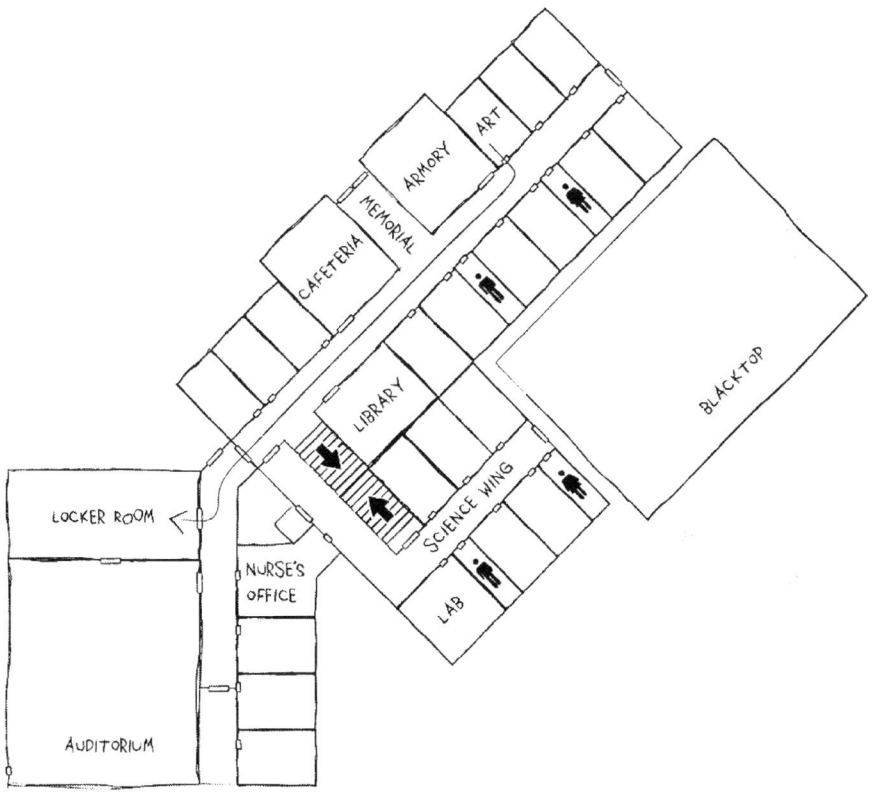

The whole campus was covered with new hand-painted posters, probably made by students. They said things like, "Quiet Zone," and, "Keep Your Voice Down." The one that stood out the most was of a frightened face with tape over its mouth that said, "Silence is golden, but duct tape is silver."

Near the main entrance, next to the cafeteria, there was a big, green star with a wood carving of a snarling tiger, the school mascot. Underneath that the trophy cases were pushed aside and hundreds of brass nameplates were mounted to the wall. It was a memorial. The image sent shivers through my body.

Thornton was a small town of about 3,000 people, and almost everyone went to Thornton Middle School at some point. In all the honor rolls, student governments, sports teams, and chess clubs, almost everyone's name had been engraved somewhere at least once.

At some point, the survivors had started prying nameplates off all those plaques and trophies, sorting and mounting them on the wall. On the left were plates mounted under the heading "Companions." Staci's plate was on that list. It read, "Staci Jingshu: Tiger Squad." Companions were refugees. There were seventy-three, and my name at the end made seventy-four. It read "Max Hartwell: Egg-ceptional work!" It was from the award I won for the egg drop.

The next heading was "Unfortunates." That section looked the most like a memorial, with personal items and handwritten prayers pinned next to the names. Milton Hall. Yanira Serrano. James Boyd. Kelly Thomas. Keith Vidal. Aiyana Jones. I stopped at Aiyana's name. Her nameplate wasn't engraved, but handwritten with a photo beside it. She was seven, not even old enough to have attended Thornton Middle School. They were the confirmed dead, which included some creepers I'd seen in the yard. There were far more Unfortunates than Companions.

The third heading had more than twice the other two combined. In fact, the names went all the way to the floor, and the rest were left in a basket on the ground. I assumed it represented those who were unaccounted for. It was labeled "Absent."

I scanned the names until I found Rich Hartwell, and moved his plate from Absent to Unfortunates. I thought back to my neighbors at Lochshire. Mr. Romero had moved to Thornton recently and didn't have a plate. No one here knew him. I found plates for Karen, Helen, and Harry Cooper. I moved them to the Unfortunates list. Karen's plate read "Soccer Champion" under her name, and so did

Harry's. I found six Burke plates, but I didn't know the first names of the judge or his wife. I noticed "Livia Burke" under Companions.

I searched for other PorcScouts, but most of them were homeschooled and didn't have nameplates. I found my best friends, Jack Freeman and Bobby Wilson. They were under Absent. The PorcScouts weren't here, but not dead either. Not for sure, at least.

There was a felt marker in the basket, so I grabbed a blank plate and wrote "Ellie." I didn't know her last name so I wrote "Green," like her eyes. I put her plate under Companions, next to mine.

There were two other handwritten names, at the very top: "Private Wozzeck" and "Major Winters."

On my first trip to the locker room, Mr. Ash was waiting in the coach's office with a clipboard. He taught math and history before the collapse. I guess that made him the accountant.

"Size?" he blurted.

"Size?" I asked.

"Your uniform. What size uniform?"

"Medium, I guess."

"Well, is it medium, or isn't it?"

"Definitely medium," I nodded.

He grabbed a bundle of folded clothes off a shelf and shoved them in my arms. Then he noted my answer on his clipboard.

I unfolded the clothes. It was a Thornton Middle School P.E. uniform. A pair of orange sweats, and a gray shirt with a tiger head on the front. The name "Palmer" was written across the back, but I didn't know who that was.

"Shoes?"

"Shoes?" I asked.

"Son, if you're going to repeat everything I ask, we're going to be here until rabbits lay eggs. What size shoes?"

"Oh. Eight."

He grabbed a pair of sneakers off another shelf and handed them to me. "Here's the procedure. You put your dirty clothes in the bin near the shower entrance, and you take a clean uni from the bin near the exit."

"But I'm not Palmer." I held up the shirt. "I'm Hartwell."

"No, you're Medium." He tapped his clipboard. "You're allowed two unis at a time—one on your back and one in your locker. You switch off every day. You shower twice a week. Random inspections are about once a week. Capish?"

"Inspections?"

"Yeah, we open up all the lockers and poke around. You'd be surprised what these kids are hiding."

I nodded.

"Now, let's get you a locker."

The room was filled with rows of standing lockers, and each locker had a combination lock built into the door, but the school had a master key that opened them all. Mr. Ash showed me the clipboard, flipped to a page that was a crude map of the room. Half the lockers had names assigned to them and half were blank.

"Take your pick."

"What's wrong with my old locker?"

"I don't know. Maybe you got friends or something you want to be next to. Besides, whatever was left in the lockers from before was emptied out and put in rotation.

I looked over the map and recognized a handful of names, but none I'd call friends. One locker in the back row was crossed out with an "X."

"What's that?" I pointed.

"The lock is busted on that one. I'd have someone fix it, but there's no shortage of empty lockers at the moment. It's a low priority."

That was what I needed. Nothing in this place was private. The lockers were not secure. I was always supervised, even when I showered. But, a locker assigned to nobody was the perfect hiding place. The lockers on each side were already taken, but the one behind it, in the next row over, was unclaimed. If I could figure a way to get access to the inside of the broken locker through the back of my locker it'd be like a secret compartment. The perfect place to begin building up an emergency supply. It was a safe place where no one else looked.

Chapter Fourteen: Thornhaven

At the end of the week, Nurse Mills gave me one last medical examination and agreed I was healthy enough to be released from quarantine. She was excited about the General Assembly and eager for me to join.

We went to the auditorium after the first bell. The bleachers were extended in half the room. The other half was filled with rows of cots where kids were sleeping. All the students were dressed in P.E. uniforms. More refugees came from classrooms and the faculty lounge upstairs.

There were about fifty refugees spread around the room. If the Companions list was accurate, the rest must be somewhere else in the school.

Nurse Mills walked me to my cot, where my survival gear bag was waiting. She said I could come to her if I needed anything, and left me to get settled. Then she went to the bleachers and sat with Ms. Lessard and Mr. Ash.

I sat on my cot and looked through my gear bag. In the front pouch, I found an emergency blanket, a water bottle, a roll of duct tape, my sewing kit, my signal mirror, a couple MREs, my family photo, and three packs of Mr. Romero's tomato seeds. I was surprised they'd left all of this, but they took Dad's research, his zPad, and my *PorcScouts Survival Guide*. My utility belt was rolled up in the main pouch, but it was empty. They had taken all the medical supplies.

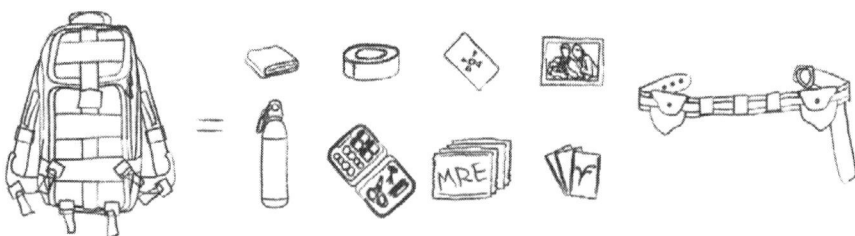

I needed to start a new bug-out bag from scratch. *Why didn't they take the tomato seeds? Didn't they have a plan to grow food?*

The kids around me were whispering and pointing at me.

"They still think you're infected." It was Staci, assigned to the cot next to me. She was a year older than me, with jet-black hair with orange tips. She wore her cheer jersey under her P.E. shirt, and sat in a wheelchair. That was new.

She eyed the MREs, so I gave her one. "Here. As a thanks for keeping me company in solitary confinement."

"Really?" She took it. "Thanks!" She tucked it in her book bag. "You shouldn't flash these around. We're not supposed to keep personal food."

Then why'd they leave it in my bag? I wondered.

Her eyes pointed to the wall behind me. On the ceiling was a black, reflective dome behind clear plastic. It was a school security camera. "Just don't get caught."

"Are the cameras still on?" I asked.

Her eyes pointed up to my left. The security office was on the second floor, and had a window that overlooked the auditorium, where Officer Pike once monitored the security screens. I could tell by the shadows that someone was there.

Miss Styx burst into the room, waving a piece of gray fabric over her head. "Attention! Attention! Everyone, gather 'round. I have exciting news!"

Conversations died down, and everyone went to the bleachers. Most people seemed eager to begin, but Sheriff Nap and Ms. Lessard looked annoyed.

"I know, I know," Miss Styx continued. "The General Assembly hasn't started, but I've had a powerful dream, a vision of the future! I want to share it with just the town folks before the Major arrives."

Staci glanced at the crowd around Miss Styx. "We should get over there. Can you give me a hand?"

"Oh, of course," I jumped up and started pushing her wheelchair.

"No, genius! I can push myself." She pointed with her eyes again, this time at my gear bag, which was in her way.

"Oh, sorry." I moved it, and we filed into the crowd.

Miss Styx stood near the bleachers and everyone circled around her. I searched the faces, but didn't see Ellie. I didn't see Mrs. Mills either, so maybe they were in the nurse's office. Miss Styx began.

* * *

Companions, some of you have heard about my vision, but I want you all to know that I think of you like family. We've all been through a terrible ordeal. We've all lost people. We're all suffering. But I've been your guidance counselor for many years. I watched most of you grow up. I love you all, and I would die for this community.

Companions, we've all been affected in some way by this plague, and we're all struggling just to keep enough food in the cafeteria. But I swear to you, life doesn't have to be miserable and short. We don't have to forget joy or purpose. We can still build decent lives for ourselves, and we don't have to live in fear. I know it's hard to imagine when we have to scavenge for everything, but I swear to you I have seen it!

I have seen a future where we have all we need to live in safety and comfort, where we grow enough food in the warm months to prepare for the cold ones. I have seen a future where a thousand Companions thrive here, and survivors flock to us; where we are prosperous and free; where we have classes, kindergarten through twelfth; where our children learn to grow healthy and strong. Most importantly, I have seen that we already have all we need to build that future, if we only seize it!

We have fertile soil, all the building materials we need, and we have this beautiful community. But

56

we also have something the future does not, and it's holding us back.

Fear is the real enemy! We let it paralyze us. We let it prevent us from achieving our potential. Defeat fear, and there's no limit to what this community can accomplish. When I think only of myself, I am scared, but knowing we are all in this together, I am not afraid. I don't know how long it will take, but I know that we must commit our spirits to the destruction of fear, and devote ourselves to the wellbeing of those who come after us.

I call this future Thornhaven, where all survivors are Companions, and all Companions are equal.

* * *

Everyone cheered.

Miss Styx unfurled her gray fabric to reveal a hand-sewn flag. There was a ring of brown thorns with a patch of green in it, and the letter "T" in the middle.

"I saw this in my dream. It's the flag of Thornhaven," explained Miss Styx. "The gray field symbolizes the granite that covers New Hampshire. The green symbolizes the prosperity we will grow here, and the ring of thorns symbolizes the Companions who band together to protect each other. In my dream, I also heard the Anthem of Thornhaven. I don't sing very well, but once you've learned the words, you can sing it better." She cleared her throat and began. Her voice was hoarse as she sang to the tune of "Darling Clementine."

> *We Companions, We Companions,*
> *Stand together by the pyre,*
> *And enjoy common salvation*
> *In the safety of the brier.*
>
> *In the valley, of the mountain,*
> *Fight together in the wreath*
> *To defend our fields of Thornton*
> *From the forest of hands and teeth.*
>
> *For our haven we will struggle.*
> *Work together, never tire.*
> *Equal rights and equal duties.*
> *Peace among us, in the Shire.*

The crowd clamored with excitement. Once Miss Styx finished, most had already picked up the words and began singing. By the third round, everyone belted out the Anthem of Thornhaven in clumsy unison.

"Hey!" A man in an unbuttoned olive green army coat leaned out the window of the security office. "Keep your damn voices down!"

The security office lights went out. Moments later, two men in army fatigues came in. One wore civilian clothes, except for his boots and army coat. Various pins and patches identified him as a ranking officer. He looked to be in his mid-forties with a touch of gray, ice-blue eyes, and a square jaw. He looked familiar.

The second wore Army-issued cargo pants tucked in his boots. His white t-shirt was blotchy with old stains, forming an outline of a combat vest he wasn't wearing. He was in his twenties with bright red hair and an unkempt beard. He was the larger of the two. On his belt were two leather holsters. One held a Sig Sauer P228. I recognized it because that model had been Dad's favorite pistol. The other held a large combat knife.

I leaned in and whispered to Staci, "Who are they?"

"Major Winters and Private Wozzeck. They showed up about a week ago from the Capitol. They're in charge now."

The Major began in an assertive, but diminished tone. "If you people want to hang your stupid flag, sing your silly nursery rhyme, and give your sappy, desperate speeches, I've got no problem with that." His voice was familiar. I knew him from somewhere. "But let's get one thing straight. I'm in charge of security, and I will not tolerate violations of the sound ordinances!"

"Major Winters! Major Winters!" Miss Styx waved her hand in the air.

"Miss Styx, would you kindly shut your trap?" He composed himself, pinching the bridge of his nose and rolled his wrist like, *get on with it.*

Miss Styx continued in her phony school counselor voice. "We have a new Companion with us today."

The Major looked annoyed by the word, "Companion."

"I thought we should all take a minute to let him introduce himself." She excitedly motioned me to the center. "Everyone, I want you all to say hello to Max." She put her hands on my shoulders and turned me toward the group.

I stood there awkwardly as the kids who remembered the ritual chanted back in unison, "Hi, Max." Most didn't bother. She had also done this on my first day of school. I was the homeschooled kid, and she treated me like a wild animal that was finally being domesticated.

"Max has been outside for a long time, but Nurse Mills says he's okay to join the group, so I want everyone to make an effort to make him feel welcome."

I saw familiar faces. There was a lot of grief in the room. I saw Scott Pike, the school bully, surrounded by his toadies, dressed in red sashes that read "Student Patrol." They sized me up.

"Max, why don't you tell us about yourself? You can start by telling us your favorite after-school activity." I gave her a disbelieving look that flustered her. "Uh, okay, why don't you tell us what you'd like to be when you grow up?"

The entire scene was odd. "Well, my dad was a scientist, but..." I quaked inside, but tried not to show it. "My mom was a pediatrician, before she died. I guess I'd like to do that, if people still have babies." I hoped they didn't hear the tremble in my voice.

A woman in the second row gasped. She covered her mouth, and the man next to her put his arm around her. She was visibly pregnant, her other hand resting on her stomach. I recognized them from Judge Burke's family photos. It was Livia and Andre.

Miss Styx broke the awkward silence. "Okay, who wants to volunteer to be Max's buddy, and make him feel at home?"

Scott raised his hand. "Pick me, Miss Styx. I'll make sure he learns his place around here real quick." He smirked as the Student Patrol snickered.

Private Wozzeck erupted in hyena-like laughter. Everyone looked at him. Winters slapped the smile off his face, and yanked him close by his shirt, whispering something.

Staci raised her hand, snapping her fingers to get their attention. "I'll show him around."

"Great!" exclaimed the Major. "New Kid has a tour guide. Everybody's happy." He motioned for Miss Styx and me to take a seat.

60

"Now, let's get down to brass tax. We've been waiting for the first snow for a long time, and I know it's been difficult, so I'll make this quick. We all got jobs to do. For starters, there's gonna be another correction in the rations."

The crowd groaned.

"I know, I know. Don't worry, it's temporary. First snow means there's gonna be some changes around here. The Capitol says cold slows down the meat puppets."

Miss Styx cleared her throat and raised her hand.

"Sorry. I meant *Unfortunates*." He spoke in a bitterly sarcastic tone as he made an exaggerated bow in her direction. "In the meantime, I want to train some good men so when the time comes, we can clear the yard."

"What?!" Sheriff Nap stood up. "Those people are our friends and family. My wife's out there! They're sick. They need our help. You can't just slaughter them like you're trimming hedges."

"Pure, naive sentiment!" The Major raised his voice. "Maybe you haven't seen those things up close, but I have. This ain't some measles epidemic, Sheriff. We're at war, and the rules of war are simple. We secure a perimeter and eliminate the threat."

Sheriff Nap responded, "The threat is manageable. It's cruel to kill them when we're so close to a cure. We should be forming search parties and bringing back survivors. That's the priority."

"Maybe you haven't noticed, but the barracks are getting pretty full, and we're running out of supplies. We need to get you all back in the refugee tents. Then we can roll out the red carpet for every Bunker Bob in town."

"We should be searching for more food in town, not wasting manpower clearing space we don't need!"

"Or maybe everything in town has already been looted. Right now, we need a sure thing. There are supplies in the yard, just waiting for us to take them."

The Sheriff started to respond, but the Major cut him off. "Shut your trap, Sheriff! You may have built this little mountain resort but I commandeered it. I'm the ranking military officer here!" Spittle flew off his lower lip as he talked. "I'm the one with orders from the Capitol!"

61

He paused and took a moment to assess the crowd. The mood was mixed.

"There's only one question, Sheriff. Are you gonna follow orders, or are we gonna have a problem?"

Sheriff Nap scanned the frightened townspeople. "No problem here, Major." He took his seat.

"That's what I thought. Now, I want…"

Thump! Thump!

The crowd fell silent; all eyes went to the rear door. Private Wozzeck looked to Major Winters for direction. The Major gave him hand signals I roughly understood as telling him to go to a window near the ceiling, above the door. Wozzeck bound up the bleachers, oddly silent, undid the latch, and swung open the window, peeking out. He signaled to the Major what I could only assume meant one creeper, and no others nearby.

The Major relaxed as he walked to the door. "Damn it, people, what have I said about inside voices? We can't be drawing every meat puppet out there down on us. Woz, help me take care of this thing."

The Private leapt off the bleachers and drew his knife. The Major pulled a Beretta M9 pistol out of his coat and a ring of keys from his pocket. He kissed a rabbit's foot keychain, and unlocked the door.

"Wait!" Miss Styx ran to the Major. "Don't do this here. Not now." She grabbed his arm and pulled him away from the door. "Some of the children haven't been outside. Please, don't spoil their innocence!"

"Ain't nobody innocent left in this world." He shrugged her off and swung the door open. A gust of cold air blew in. He grabbing the creeper by its sweater and threw it into the room. It fell on its face and slid across the floor, leaving a trail of brown muck behind it.

It was a teen girl, sprinkled with snow. The Major rolled his eyes. He holstered his M9 and motioned for Woz to hand him the knife. The girl began pushing itself up and he pounced on its back, pinning it down.

"This is a school, ain't it? Well, here's lesson one." The girl moaned and gurgled as he pulled off its ski cap and yanked its head up by the hair.

"Amy!" A woman screamed and ran toward them.

The Major motioned to Woz, who held the woman back.

"Please don't!" she cried. "She's my little girl!"

"Let's get one thing straight," the Major continued. "This *thing* is *not* your little girl. It doesn't play tea time. It doesn't care what Billy said about Courtney. It doesn't need help studying math. It's a damn meat puppet! And the only thing to do with meat puppets is cut the strings!"

He shoved its face to the ground, and put the knife tip at the base of its skull. He pushed down on the knife, driving it in slow so everyone could see. Blood pooled on the ground underneath them. "Right behind the eyes, right between the ears. That's the kill zone."

The girl began convulsing. He gave the knife a quick quarter-turn and the girl went limp, spraying blood in his face.

"No!" The mother fell to her knees.

People freaked! Children cried. Adults were visibly horrified. Ms. Lessard had an inquisitive look I'd only seen when Dad was on the brink of a breakthrough with his work.

The Major patted the body down and emptied its pockets on the ground, frowning when he found nothing useful. He deadlifted the girl. Woz opened the door and the Major hurled the limp corpse into the snow. He came back to the group, his face still marked with the girl's blood.

"I want every able-bodied male over fifteen to report to the Armory tomorrow after the first bell. This is a draft. No-shows will get half-rations for a week. I'll pick my team based on performance. As for the rest of you, I don't care what you do. Just keep your voices down. Class dismissed!"

Despite his goose stepping, Winters couldn't deprive the people of a day of rest, so Staci and I had the rest of the day to tour Thornhaven.

Some people routinely stayed after the General Assembly for an impromptu spiritual service. No one had any formal religious training, so the responsibility fell on a man named Moses. He was an old man with dark skin and gray hair. He looked South Asian, but his drawl was Caribbean.

> *Yuh tink de world change so much? Is de same as always. People livin juss as long as God gih dem. Deat visit us every day, same as always. Only ting is we used to pretend dat it wasn't comin. Used to hide deat away. We was livin a lie. Allyuh bawlin nah cause you got bit by dis nasty trut. Dyin is juss part of livin, same as always. Deat knockin down walls. Climbin up towers. Dats real! Yuh eh go live forever, so you go have to decide what yuh livin for.*
>
> *Dem jumbies out dere eh so different from allyuh in here. Dey juss livin out God's plan, same as always. People bin chewin on eachuddah fuh a long time. Dey juss more honest bout it nah. People bin tiefin, an backbitin, and killin each udder since Cain bury Abel. Ah tink God juss showin us what we always was, and why we got to strive to be bettah.*

Stacy said that Moses was the Pine Grove Cemetery groundskeeper before the collapse. That gave him a lot of quiet time to think, and showed him firsthand how death impacted the living. It gave him a unique credibility on spiritual matters. The school janitor was in the yard, so Moses took up his duties. He was laid back, never rushed, never anxious, and his sing-song inflection made it contagious. He was content doing the work that was never finished, and always willing to stop his rounds to tell stories from his well-traveled life, which drew crowds. That was how he became the interim town chaplain.

The school looked the same, except for the boarded windows and reinforced doors. They mounted segments of chain-link fencing inside so hallways could be blocked if the building was infiltrated by creepers. That was smart, but it looked like a prison.

Staci showed me the library, which doubled as a classroom. There weren't enough students or teachers left for regular classes, so all grade levels were taught in one room. She said we'd restart class Monday morning.

We went to the cafeteria, which was run by students on kitchen duty during meals. The freezer and pantry were padlocked to prevent snacking between meals.

We couldn't go upstairs because the only wheelchair access was the broken freight elevator, and because only adults were allowed upstairs. Single adults were paired up in the upstairs classrooms, and families stayed in the downstairs classrooms. We couldn't go in the boiler room because it was off-limits except for Ms. Lessard, Moses, and the Major.

The administrative office was commandeered by the Major and was used by the Watchers and Runners as an Armory. There was at least one Watcher on the roof at all times. Runners went out in teams during the day.

Staci said the only way out of the building was the zip line on the roof. It was pretty ingenious. One zip line went from the roof of the auditorium to a BEARCAT outside the fence, and the other went from a telephone pole across the street to the roof of the Armory. That way, the Runners completely avoided the creepers in the yard, but it was the only escape.

I asked her about the wheelchair.

I was in Mr. Ash's math class when the lockdown alarm went off. I was initially happy about getting out of a pop quiz. They brought us to the auditorium to take roll, and said it was a drill, but we saw the emergency vehicles outside. Panic spread fast. They wouldn't tell us anything except that they called our parents.

The faculty kept us in the auditorium until our parents arrived, but when they came, the police wouldn't let them leave, either. Families were put in the Health Department's refugee tents. My mom works at the New Hampshire State House in Concord and they had a pandemic to deal with, so she couldn't just leave. If nobody came for us, they left us in the auditorium. They brought us cots and blankets. We've been living in there ever since.

For the first week, emergency broadcasts told everyone to get whatever emergency supplies they had and come to the school. But all the activity drew the walkers. Police blocked off the streets with barricades, and patrolled the fence to keep everyone safe.

Miss Styx is always worried about people's spirit. She asked people to call them "Unfortunates." It's supposed to be respectful, I guess. I think it's stupid. We had plenty of food in the beginning, so she organized a big community barbeque. That weekend, we were supposed to play soccer against Gilman Middle School, but it was cancelled, so we played students vs. faculty at the barbeque.

We didn't have a whole cheer squad, so I got promoted to captain! It was fun but stupid. We should've known better. The noise attracted more walkers from town, so the police doubled their patrols out front. Everything was under control.

No one expected one of those things to wander in from the woods behind the school. We don't even know how it got through the fence, but it only took one for everyone to freak. It chomped on someone in the back row, and that started a stampede.

I got trampled.

I woke up in the medical tent with a severe spinal injury. Lucky for me, we still had doctors in camp at the time, but the problems didn't end there. The screaming drew more walkers from the woods, and when the police shot them, it drew more from town. It didn't happen all at once, but they came in waves, sometimes days apart. I was bedridden but I could hear the gunshots. The bigger the firefight, the bigger the next wave, until the walkers overran the barricades.

Sheriff Nap saved me. He carried me from the medical tent to the auditorium and locked me inside with the other kids. The walkers would have taken over the whole school if it weren't for him. Everyone alive owes their life to him, but we lost so many.

That's how I got my wheelchair. It belonged to some old guy who died.

The police cleared the hallways and reinforced the windows and doors. We were safe inside. We ate the food from the cafeteria. We had heat and shelter, but we were trapped. The yard was overrun, and the adults decided to wait for the government to find a cure, rather than kill the walkers. After a couple weeks, we were running out of supplies.

They couldn't bury the bodies, so they burned them in the furnace. People were mad about using dead bodies for heat, but we didn't have a choice.

It's a good thing, too, because the smoke is how the Capitol found us.

Major Winters and Private Woz were flying a scout helicopter from the Capitol. They found us about a week ago. The Major made radio contact with the Capitol to coordinate a rescue effort. He even contacted the refugee center in Concord. My parents are alive! I'll be taken there when it's safe. Major Winters trained the Watchers to patrol the roof instead of the fence, so they could spare men for other tasks. Private Woz set up the zip lines and trained the Runners to bring back supplies. They really saved us. They even set up the bell schedule.

* * *

"I've been wondering about the bells," I interrupted. "Doesn't that attract the walkers?"

Staci smirked at her watch. "Follow me."

We went down the math and science wing. She crashed into the door of the girl's bathroom and it flew open. She rolled in, but I stopped.

"Come on, nobody's in this part of the school." She waved me in. "I want to show you something."

I followed her in and she went into the handicapped stall. I leaned in to look.

She checked her watch and waved to hurry me in. "Look," she whispered, pointing to a small window above the toilet.

I stepped on the seat and peered out. It was the blacktop behind the school. I saw the basketball hoops, tetherball poles, and the playground. To the right, there were refugee tents swarming with creepers. The fence enclosing the back of the school was knocked down and creepers wandered in and out of the woods.

The cold was slowing them down. Some were clawing at the refugee tents, or wandering in the field. A group was reaching for a black bird perched on the monkey bars.

"What's going on?" I whispered.

"Just watch."

The lunch bell went off, giving us five minutes to get to the cafeteria.

Creepers all over the yard stopped what they were doing and headed toward the building. The distracted ones followed when they saw the majority shuffling in the same direction.

I thought they'd press right up against the wall, but they didn't. They all stopped a few feet from the building, like a wall of bodies at the edge of the blacktop.

I looked at Staci. "Why are they doing that?"

She grinned. "Because they remember."

The creepers formed crooked lines on the classroom numbers painted on the ground, like we used to do after recess.

"Why do the adults do it?" I asked.

"They went to this school, too, or some school. I guess years and years of bell schedules really leaves an impression. When they forget about food, they just do whatever they remember doing. That, or they're just following the others when they line up."

Officer Pike came so close to the window it startled me. I could smell the brain rot. It walked up and down the line, patrolling like when he was alive.

"Watch this," she added, looking at her watch and pointing as the second bell rang.

One by one, the creepers wandered away.

"Every day, they line up, and every day, lose interest, and go back to the yard. It's a routine. We're safe as long as nothing riles them up." She wheeled out of the stall. "Now, let's eat."

Chapter Seventeen: Rations

The cafeteria looked the same, except there were fewer kids. They lined up at the trough with their trays, as volunteers scooped out gray slop. Charred meat cubes were molded out of processed pink slime that was stored in a vat that looked like a barrel of industrial waste, except that it was technically protein, which was better than nothing. It was served smothered in ketchup, which they claimed was a vegetable. They also served sealed bags of pretzels. It wasn't very appetizing, and a lot of mystery meat ended up in the trash to the dismay of faculty.

The staff made every attempt to get the kids to eat everything served to them, but punishments only led to increasingly clever ways of disposing of the tough little bricks. As a result, Thornhaven had a serious rat problem, which some argued would be a preferable source of protein.

Kids were seated at separate tables in cliques. Geeks, jocks, hipsters, and emo kids, just like before. Staci moved toward the popular kids' table. What was left of the cheer squad was there with other athletes from school. There were also high school kids now, preppy looking teenagers with expensive clothes and perfect hair. The older boys flicked paper footballs back and forth, and snickered when they landed in someone's food, while older girls filed their nails, and looked at themselves in compact mirrors as they gossiped disapprovingly about everything.

I'd never sat with the popular kids before. I didn't have anything in common with them, and it was as awkward now as it would have been before.

As we approached, they started shushing each other. The chatter went silent. Staci didn't sit with them, and as she passed by, one of the older boys made a loud farting noise in the pit of his elbow. Then one of the girls yelled, "Gross! Staci, that's disgusting!"

The table erupted in cruel laughter, but Staci ignored them and moved on.

"I thought those were your friends?" I asked.

"The captain of the Tiger Squad was popular," she said. "The girl in the wheelchair is not."

We went to the back table with other kids from the auditorium. For them, the former playground social order had been disrupted because they were bound by more than fashion or music. Grief made them outcasts, but they didn't share any other interests, so we ate in silence. It was an in-group of outsiders.

Then there was Scott and the Student Patrol. There was no more lunch money to steal, or any place to spend it if there was, but that didn't stop them from terrorizing smaller kids. After I sat down, Scott and his crew surrounded us.

"Hartwell, you're new here, so I hope Staci told you the rule."

"What rule is that?" I asked.

"Show up late, lose your plate." He popped one of my meat nuggets in his mouth.

Everyone kept their heads down and watched with sideways glances. I tried standing up, but two toadies pushed me back down.

"Come on, Scott!" Staci protested. "He didn't know."

"Ignorance is no excuse," he grinned.

I turned toward him. "You can't just take my food. I have to eat."

"Oh, I'm not gonna take your food," he leaned down so his greasy breath brushed my cheek. "You're gonna give it to me."

I looked around, but there was no support, except Staci. Nothing was going to stop him. I sighed, and handed him my tray.

He pocketed the pretzels, and passed the rest of the tray to the Student Patrol, who grabbed for their fair share, like creepers fighting for scraps. Then he picked Staci's tray up.

I grabbed the edge of her tray. "Scott," I barked, "what's wrong with you? People are dying, and you're stealing food from orphans?" I almost choked on the word. It was the first time I'd said it out loud.

The room fell silent as everyone turned and watched.

"Rules are rules!" Scott pulled the tray; but I didn't let go. I yanked it downward and let go, sling-shotting the slop in his face.

The crowd jeered, even the Student Patrol laughed. It quickly escalated into an uproar as the whole room banged on the tables, cheering for a fight. Scott scooped the goop out of his eyes as his gang circled around.

In another life, I would've run home, but now we were locked in the school together. There was nowhere to escape where he couldn't find me. I was terrified, but I accepted it. I'd take a beating rather than fight. Maybe he'd leave me alone if I went limp.

Scott reached way back and planted his fist in my chest and knocked me back. I skipped a breath, but I didn't go down. I took it.

He looked as surprised as I was. I was tough, at least in the middle.

He swung again, but I sidestepped, giving him a quick pop in the nose. No strength there, but at least I connected. I backed away several steps to think for a moment. That just enraged him. He roared and charged with clenched fists.

I flashed back to the first day of the outbreak. My dad—that thing—charging at me. I looked for something to defend myself and spotted a chair. I roughly guessed the speed and distance, the necessary force, and torque. But this situation didn't call for a catapult. It called for a club.

I lifted the chair and swung hard, bashing Scott's head with a loud *crack*. Scott went barreling through the crowd and face-first into a trash can.

There was one brief triumphant moment between winning the fight and the Student Patrol knocking me down, kicking, and punching. My last thought was that this must be what it looks like to be taken down by creepers; then everything went dark.

Chapter Eighteen: Open Wounds

I came to when the furnace kicked on. A gust of warm air blew out of the vents. I worried, if they used dead bodies for heat, could the virus be in the air, or would the fire destroy it? If there was a risk, they'd know by now... wouldn't they?

I recognized the overhead lights. I was in the nurse's office.

I spotted my empty trauma kit in the trash. I felt the anger growing in my gut. First aid supplies were a critical part of a good bug-out bag. I started searching drawers for supplies, but stopped. If I stole from them, was that any better than their stealing from me? The injured person who ended up needing the supplies probably wouldn't be the person who stole them from me, anyway. I decided to take only what was mine, and only when they had plenty of their own. I didn't want them to notice anything missing.

I grabbed an elastic tourniquet band, some sterile pads, bandages, tweezers, some safety pins, ibuprofen, adhesive tape, alcohol wipes, butterfly sutures, burn gel, and the most important part of my kit—the instructions. I only took one thing not originally in my kit—a tube of antibiotic ointment. To think, if we'd had it earlier, Ellie wouldn't be sick, and we wouldn't be stuck in this place. I refilled my trauma kit and tucked it under my shirt. I'd stash it in my locker for now, but I had to figure out how to get into the hidden compartment before the first inspection.

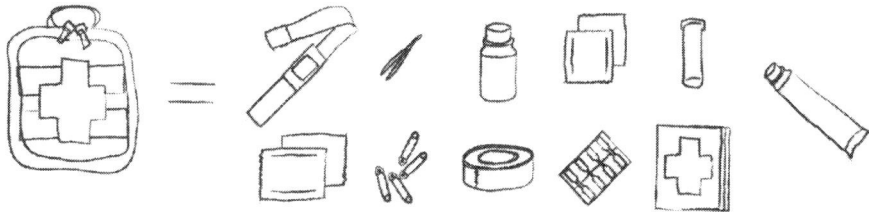

I opened the door and went into the main office. Nurse Mills was setting Scott's nose. I had busted it open pretty bad. He sobbed as she crunched it back into place, and I cringed. I felt sorry for him.

"Oh, good. You're awake," she said. "How're you feeling?"

"My ribs hurt," I winced.

"You're bruised up, but nothing's broken." She bandaged Scott's nose she and told him, "If anyone asks, tell them you slipped during your patrol. You two are lucky I stopped the fight before anyone else saw. You know the punishment for fighting is quarantine." She pointed to two plates on the counter. We sat down to eat.

"I want you two to apologize."

"I'm sorry, Mrs. Mills," Scott said, still chewing. "It'll never happen again."

"Not to me, Scott. To Max."

Scott looked to me with a stern brow. Then he smiled, bits of black meat in his teeth, "That was pretty gutsy, Hartwell. I didn't think you had it in you."

"You had it coming."

He chuckled. "I can respect that." He held out his hand. "I think we better be friends, otherwise we might kill each other."

I eyed him skeptically. He sounded legit. I shook his hand, and pulled him close. "Not just me. You're going to leave all of us alone. We're all in this together. We're all orphans now."

Scott laughed. "Speak for yourself, Orphan Boy. My dad's not dead. He's on a special mission for the Major, delivering everyone's votes to the Capitol."

"What? That's not true." I insisted. "He's in the yard."

Scott scowled. "You're a liar."

Nurse Mills' eyes went wide. "That can't be right!" She fidgeted with her hair. "Why, we expect Officer Pike back any day now. If he was in the yard, the Watchers would have seen him." She gave me a look that begged me to play along. "Max, that was a mean thing to say. Tell Scott you didn't mean it. Tell him it was a joke."

I said nothing.

"That's pretty messed up, Hartwell." Scott said. "I don't think that's funny at all."

"Scott, why don't you head back the auditorium," she said. "Third period is almost over, and you have patrol duty."

He scowled at me as he left.

"Why are you lying to him?" I asked. "His dad is out there. I saw him."

She gasped in frustration. "Max, Scott is a very fragile boy, with a lot of behavioral problems. If you think he was challenging before, you can't imagine what it's taken for him to adjust to life here. Losing his father would devastate him. There's no telling how he'd lash out. It's best for everyone if he goes on thinking his dad is on an important mission."

"But it's only a matter of time. He'll be angrier when he finds out."

"That's why you can't tell anybody! No one knows except the Major's men and a few of the faculty."

"What's the point in deceiving everyone else?"

"Democracy," she answered plainly. "People have to believe their vote matters, and the system still works. They have to feel like they're part of something. It keeps them going. Hope is all that's holding this community together. Without that, we'd have anarchy."

I nodded, though something didn't sound right. I glanced around the room. "Where's Ellie? Shouldn't she be here?"

Her expression went cold. "Max, I'm so sorry. I didn't want to be the one to tell you."

"Tell me what?" I had already guessed.

"I didn't want you to worry while you were recuperating."

"Tell me what?!"

"Her wounds were just too severe." She fidgeted with her hair. "The blood poisoning..."

"When?" I scowled.

"She was taken to the boiler room on Wednesday."

I felt the blood rush out of my face, and thought I might be sick. I looked up to the heating vents, and for the first time I wasn't worried *what* I was breathing, but *whom*.

Chapter Nineteen: An Unexpected Guest

Before the first morning bell, I was startled awake by rustling at my feet. I reached down and felt fur, and heard a familiar sound.

"Stinky!" I bolted upright.

The other kids groaned, but I didn't care. I pulled him close as he rubbed his forehead against my cheek.

"How'd you get in here?" I whispered. "How did you find me?"

Stinky purred. He was cold, damp, and I could feel his ribs. He'd been underfed.

"I'm sorry," I said. "I don't have any food for you, but breakfast is soon. We can find you something."

A flashlight shined in my face. "Who are you talking to?" asked Staci.

Stinky tensed and hissed.

"Turn that off," I whispered, pushing the light away. "You're freaking him out."

"You have a cat!" she exclaimed. "Where'd he come from? What's his name?"

"Keep it down. His name is Stinky. I saved him, or maybe he saved me, sort of. It's a long story."

"Cute!" she giggled.

"Shut up!"

"Is he hungry? I have some belt cheese?" She rummaged through her book bag.

"What the heck is belt cheese?"

"It's mozzarella, packaged and strung together like belt-fed ammo." She pulled a bundle out of her pack and unfurled six sticks of white cheese. "We call them cheese cartridges."

"I thought hoarding food was against the rules?"

"Everyone does it. It's money now." She ripped a stick off, and peeled the plastic. "Do you want it or not?" Stinky immediately leapt on her lap and sniffed her offering.

"Isn't cheese bad for cats?" I asked.

"Sort of. They love it, but it gives them diarrhea when they're old. How old is he?"

"I don't know. He's not mine."

"Well, whose is he?" she asked sarcastically.

I thought before answering. "He owns himself. Doesn't everyone?"

Stinky bit the cheese then scarfed it whole.

"I guess we'll find out," she quipped. "Don't worry, he doesn't look old." She ripped off a second cartridge and pointed it at me. "You want one?"

"Are you sure? You said it's money."

"Yeah. I owe you for the meal pack. Some people trade for food they like, but not me. I trade for calories and protein. That was some pretty dense nutrition."

"That's pretty smart."

"So take it." She tossed me the cheese cartridge and I tucked it in my gear bag.

"That's pretty smart, too," she said.

Stinky poked his head in my gear bag for the cheese. I put him in my lap.

A boy's voice came from behind. "You better hide him before the faculty sees him." Staci's flashlight shined in his face. He was scrawny, and had hair so blond it looked white and bright blue eyes.

"What will they do if they find him?" I asked.

"If you're lucky, they throw him back out in the snow, but they'll probably kill him. They're totally paranoid about anything from outside. Worst case, they'll cook him!" He was poking objects in a black digital camera case. I saw matches, cracked reading glasses, and something bundled in wax paper. It may have been chocolate. When he noticed me looking, he zipped it shut and tucked it in his jacket.

He said his name was Holland. Staci said his name was Niles. I knew him from school. Actually, I knew *them*. Holland and Niles were twins, but they couldn't be less alike. Holland played lacrosse. Niles was in the Audio-Visual club. Only one of them had survived, but it was unclear which one. To me, he was Holland Perry; he had the right to be called whatever he wanted.

We made so much noise talking that we woke the kids around us. They buzzed with excitement when they saw Stinky, which woke even more kids. Soon, everyone was crowding around us, trying to get their hands on him.

Stinky didn't like the attention, and squirmed to get out of my arms, but I held him tight as he howled and batted away their grasping hands. The morning bell rang, but it didn't distract them any. The adults would be in soon.

Stinky buried his head in my arms. I pushed the kids back and turned away from the horde.

"Wha di heck is all de ruckus in here?" It was Moses.

The kids stopped and the crowd parted as Moses moved through. He leaned down to me and whispered, "Fella, Ah tink yuh bess leh me take him. Ah swear by God dat ah keep him safe. Dais de trut, but yuh gotta leh me hide im till it safe. Wha yuh say?

He reached down and took Stinky right out of my arms. Stinky trusted him immediately. I hoped he was a good judge of people.

Chapter Twenty: Training Day

There was bustling between the morning bell and first period as people started their day—eating if they had food, showering if it was their day, changing their clothes, and trading. While I got dressed, I examined the inside of my locker to see how it was constructed. I thought if it was held together with bolts or screws I could loosen them, and slide the panel between the two lockers over. No such luck. The lockers were built out of steel sheets, and the side panels had flaps that folded in and were welded to the back panel. I'd have to come up with something more drastic.

During breakfast, the Major made the morning announcements over the PA.

> *"Good morning, Thornhaven! Today's the big day, and we've all got jobs to do. Regular classes are suspended 'till further notice. And all students are required to perform more relevant duties. New work schedules are posted outside the Armory. The rest of you should perform your regular duties with added satisfaction, knowing you're part of the war effort. The laundry team has been slacking, so let's not let that pile up. I want my sheets as white as snow. Speaking of which, we're in luck, happy campers! It's going to be a blustery day, and that means it's time for the winter harvest! I want all able-bodied men over 15 to report to the Armory for first period, and bring a jacket. We'll be training first and second period, and after lunch, we'll pick teams and start clearing the yard."*

Staci showed me to the posted schedules. My work detail for first period was Science Lab with Ms. Lessard, which was weird because classes were canceled. Even weirder, it said to go to the Faculty

Lounge, but students weren't allowed on the second floor. I went anyway, as directed and found teachers having breakfast. The cabinets were packed with supplies, and the staff waited in line as Miss Styx handed out a plastic-wrapped custard pastry from an S-Mart box. Moses was refilling a vending machine with pretzels, fruit strips, and belt cheese.

They had a vending machine!

Moses was the first to see me. He held his finger to his lips and motioned quietly to something in his pocket. He pulled out a can of sardines, just enough so I could see. I nodded, and he went back to work.

Mr. Ash saw me next. "Hey! This is for faculty only."

They rustled when they saw me, hiding their breakfast, and closing the cabinets as if I'd caught them stealing. Maybe I had. It was a lot of food for a camp where all food was rationed.

"Calm down, Jim," interrupted Ms. Lessard. "He's my new Teacher's Aid. Shouldn't you be headed to the Armory with the other men?" She patted his belly. "You'd make a great soldier if you got into fighting weight."

"And if a frog had wings, he wouldn't bump his butt when he hopped," he joked. "I went to college to avoid the draft. Why do you think I ended up a teacher?"

"Major's orders," she smiled. "You too, Moses."

"Ah don see de point," Moses stood up. "Ah got my hands full chasin dese rats in de pantry." He winked at me. "Dese bones too ol to be chasin dem jumbies out dere."

"Moses, we've all got jobs to do. The Major won't assign you anything you can't handle, but how can he know what that is if you don't go?" she insisted.

"Ahm goin, Ahm goin." He squeezed my shoulder as he left with Mr. Ash.

"Good morning, Max. Feel free to have anything you want."

The other faculty got their snacks and left for their work details. I took Staci's advice, and went for nutrition over flavor. I got two oatmeal raisin energy bars, ate one, and saved the other for later.

I was alone with Ms. Lessard.

"Good morning, Ms. Lessard?" The scene felt awkward. Next to the vending machine was a hot drink dispenser. I went to it.

"Call me Julia. We're not in class. You never belonged in my class, anyway."

"What do you mean?" The machine had spouts for hot chocolate, cappuccino, and pumpkin spice latte. I got a cup of hot chocolate.

"Come on, Max, you're too advanced for middle school science. That's why I pulled you from the volunteer pool."

The hot chocolate was so watered down it looked like weak tea. "Because you're organizing an AP science class?" I sipped it and could barely taste the cocoa, but at least it was hot.

"No, nothing so remedial. I need a lab assistant. I know you're young, but given who's left, you're the best qualified. I'd ask Mrs. Mills, but she's got her hands full just dealing with bumps and scrapes, and she doesn't have the hands-on experience you have."

"What experience?"

"You've seen the infected in the wild."

"You want to study the creepers?"

"Is that what you call them?"

"Yeah." *That's what Ellie called them.* "What do you call them?"

"People are calling them 'Unfortunates,' but if we're being scientific, I think we should call them infected."

We're all infected, I remembered Ellie saying, and tried to remember what Dad called them. "I think we should just call them subjects."

"Works for me," she said.

"And you've built a lab?" I asked.

"In a manner of speaking. So, you'll help me?"

"I don't know."

"Max, we are physicians in a time of plague. We have an obligation to do everything in our power."

I nodded.

"Great! So, have you seen how the subjects behave in the wild?" I nodded again. A concerned look crossed her face. "Have you ever been bitten?"

"No, of course not. Bites burn you up, and start the change."

"Always?"

"Yeah. I think so. I've never seen someone survive a bite. Have you?"

She considered before answering. "No."

Chapter Twenty-One: Principal Bowness

I followed Ms. Lessard to the science room, which was down an unused hallway in the back of the school. Her lab was across from the boiler room. The wooden classroom doors had a narrow window above the knob, but the boiler room door was solid steel. In an emergency, it'd hold out an army of creepers, but there probably wasn't another exit. An orange nameplate read "Authorized Personnel Only."

A dark red smear on the wall ended at the boiler room door.

"Ms. Lessard, I mean Julia, what happened to Ellie?"

She gave an apologetic look. "Max, I'm so sorry. We did everything we could, but the blood poisoning weakened her immune system, and the ataxic hyperphagia took over." She used dad's term. She must have read his research. "There wasn't time to arrange a visit, and we take care of bodies right away, to be safe. After that, we decided it would be better to let you settle in before we told you. I wanted to tell you, because I know how mature you are, but I was outvoted."

She unlocked the science lab. "Wait inside," she said, opening the door for me. "I'll be right back. I have to get something for you." Then she slipped into the boiler room.

The room was largely the same as before the outbreak, with a whiteboard, a wall-sized periodic table, and a mural of great scientists and their accomplishments: from Euclid and his geometry, to Galileo with his telescope, and Elon Musk and his Mars colony.

Lab stations filled the room, each with a Bunsen burner, eyewash station, and two stools. The teacher's station was twice as wide, with a plug strip and some additional equipment she had acquired from the Health Department. She had an electron microscope, a centrifuge, an autoclave, a standing freezer and an incubator, plus some other equipment I didn't recognize.

Dad's research was spread out on her workstation. I looked over the graphs and spreadsheets, and still understood very little, but when I read his notes, I could almost hear his voice in my head, reading them to me.

I heard metal scraping and spun around. It was coming from behind a green curtain that masked the back of the room. I pushed the edge aside to peek in.

Principal Bowness was on his knees with his hands in a metal bucket. He pulled out a living rat and shoved it in his mouth head first. I heard the crunch.

"Mr. Bowness?"

He spun around. The pale complexion and constricted pupils told me it was a creeper.

It roared and lunged at me.

I flung myself back, tripping over a lab stool.

A chain pulled tight around its neck. It was looped like the choke collar on a junkyard dog. The other end was bolted to the wall. The harder Mr. Bowness yanked, the tighter the chain cinched. I was surprised it didn't pull off its own head.

"I see you've met our first test subject." Ms. Lessard was standing right behind me. "Sorry, I should have warned you."

"Why are you keeping it here?"

"To study how it behaves, and how it thinks, if you call it thinking." She drew a taser from her workstation's top drawer. "Watch this." She zapped the taser in the air, making a loud cracking noise from the electrical charge.

Mr. Bowness froze. It didn't retreat, but it stopped pulling on its restraints. It just stood there, eyes locked on the taser, gurgling and drooling bits of rat on itself.

"You trained it!" I exclaimed. "How did you do that?"

"I tried everything. Pain compliance doesn't work. They even ignore fire, but the taser still incapacitates them. The electroshock causes involuntary muscle contractions, so they just drop, if you turn up the juice," she explained.

"But, you didn't shock it."

"I don't have to anymore. I used to zap it when it misbehaved, but it figured out that the taser caused the seizures. Now all I have to do is threaten it, and it backs down. It's not the pain. I think it doesn't like losing control."

"It learned!"

"Exactly. So, now I punish bad behavior with electroshocks, and I reward good behavior with food. Punishments and rewards are all you need to start altering behavior. It's just like training students in class. This one's responding well, so far."

"You have others?"

"Not anymore. The others didn't respond to conditioning. This one is different for some reason. I just haven't figured out why."

Ms. Lessard closed the curtain and left Mr. Bowness to its rats. We walked back to the front.

She had Ellie's book bag sitting on a table. "Normally, personal belongings like this are redistributed, but seeing as

87

you're practically her next of kin, I thought you should have it."
She handed me the book bag; I inspected it.

Ellie's first aid kit and food were gone, but a water filter, fifty
feet of paracord, and her water bottle were there. I also found her
flashlight and a road map in the front pouch.

"I have something else for you." She reached into her pocket
and pulled out my multi-tool. "This was yours, wasn't it?"

"Yes!" I grabbed it.

"I thought so. Miss Styx had logged it at the Armory as a
weapon, but no one was using it. I figured it might have some
sentimental value."

"Thank you." I nodded. "And it does. My dad gave it to me."

"Just don't flash this stuff around. You're not supposed to have
it—zero-tolerance policy, and all."

"Do you know what happened to my Survival Guide, and my
zPad?" I asked.

"Miss Styx probably shelved the Survival Guide in the library.
I held onto the zPad hoping there was more research on it."

"I printed everything but the Pigeon Experiment."

"What's the Pigeon Experiment?" she asked.

"It's a video. I used pigeons to test if Free Breeze air freshener
prevented a subject from tracking by smell."

"Did it work?"

"Sort of. That's how I avoided them outside."

"That's genius! Can you show me?" She retrieved the zPad
from her desk. "It's charged, but I can't unlock it. Do you know the
password?"

"No, but I know the security questions. Dad's middle school mascot was the Tigers. The last five digits of his driver's license were 21277, and his favorite author was my mom, Joy Hartwell."

She tapped in the answers and the zPad's screen lit up. She laughed as she scrolled through the videos I'd downloaded before I lost power. There were news broadcasts, and #BiterGram videos. She played the Pigeon Experiment video. I heard the recorded sounds of Mr. Romero chomping on the bird.

Behind the curtain, Mr. Bowness replied with a long, low moan. We traded a surprised look and both glanced to the back of the room. "Is it trying to communicate?" I asked.

"I doubt it. It's probably some primitive instinct," she answered. "Max, listen. Your dad's research has been a real game changer in my work. Major Winters has agreed to report my progress to the Capitol. If you'll help me, I bet we can crack this thing."

I had mixed feelings. I wasn't comfortable using creepers as guinea pigs, but if Ms. Lessard understood Dad's research, that was critical. I was going to be stuck there through the winter anyway, and without Ellie, there wasn't much reason to escape. "I'll help you if I can keep my zPad. It's full of family stuff I can't replace."

"No problem. I'll get you a flash drive and we can back up all the research on the school computers. As long you bring it to the lab for work, you've got a deal."

We shook on it.

"Fantastic!" she beamed. "I'll get you keys to the lab. It's important that you don't talk about what we do here. Most people just don't understand what's necessary to make scientific progress."

I nodded slowly. "What kind of progress?"

"Let me show you," she bubbled.

Ms. Lessard reached into the standing freezer and pulled out a tray of slides with time stamps. She pulled out a slide. "Frozen brain tissue." She flipped the electron microscope on, loaded the slide, and adjusted the settings. "You can see the spongiform brain damage, like your dad said." She pushed the eyepiece toward me.

I looked into microscope and saw a mass of blotchy, pink tissue. It looked like a slice of salami, peppered with black spots like tumors, and white holes where the light showed through.

"Freezing slows the infection," she said. "So, you can see the damage, but watch what happens."

I looked again, and as the slide thawed, the tissue turned to gray mush.

"The tissue is necrotic," she said. "You can see the damage, but the sample disintegrates before you can find the culprit. That's the problem your dad couldn't solve."

"But you've solved it?"

She bristled with excitement. "Everyone was looking in the brain for the active infection, but the hidden infection is airborne." She returned the brain tissue slide to the freezer, and opened the incubator, which was loaded with more trays of slides. It had an awful yeasty smell.

She pulled out another slide. "Living lung tissue."

"Living?"

"More or less. The tissue is suspended in a nutrient-rich solution, and the incubator simulates the body temperature. The cells are alive but the donor is dead."

I didn't want to know where she got it.

She loaded the slide. "Take a look."

Sure enough, the sample was alive, and it was full of the same black spots as the dead brain tissue.

"Do you see them?"

I nodded.

"Now, let me see." She swung the eye piece toward herself and adjusted the settings. "Here!" She pushed it back to me. "Look at that!"

The microscope was zoomed in to one of the black cysts. It looked like an unstable blob and after a moment it burst, releasing hundreds of little wiggling pods. They looked like leeches, crawling away from the shattered cyst. "What are they?"

"Max, your dad was brilliant, but he was a virologist. He was looking for a virus from the beginning, and he saw what he wanted to see, but it's not a virus. It's a parasite!" She opened a textbook and pointed. "It's an extremely aggressive human strain of toxoplasmosis."

The picture was similar to the slide, but not exactly the same critter. It's hard to tell with single-celled organisms, but the parasite in the book had only one nucleus, which is typical. The parasites in the slides appeared to have two.

"That doesn't make sense. Parasites aren't airborne."

"Over short distances they can be. Microscopic egg sacs gestate in the lungs and throat, and get transmitted like the flu," she explained.

"That's good news, right? Short range is good."

"I suppose. The bad news is those black tissue cysts shield them from antibiotics, radiation, and pretty much every other treatment. After a cyst bursts, a healthy immune system will fight the larva. That explains the hidden infection, but once the immune system is compromised, if the subject dies or contracts some other opportunistic infection, the larvae mature and invade the brain. That triggers the active transformation."

"What about bites?"

"I haven't tested this yet, but my theory is that the adult parasites are in the blood. Bites, scratches, or any fluid contact transmits the adult parasite, not the eggs sacs. That's why the immune system can't fight back."

I grabbed the textbook and skimmed the entry on toxoplasmosis.

Toxoplasmosis is potentially carried by all warm-blooded animals, including humans, but the primary hosts are rodents and cats. Rodents are commonly infected by ingesting feces from infected cats, and show behavioral symptoms including twitchy locomotion and reduced reflexes. Infected rodents become attracted to the smell of cats, making them easier prey. The parasite's life cycle is complete when an infected cat consumes an infected rodent, so the parasite can reproduce in the cat's intestine."

On the next page, a diagram showed the stages of the parasite's reproductive cycle, coinciding with the digestive cycle of a cat. I skipped ahead to the section on human infection.

Humans are typically infected by eating raw, infected meat, and by transmission from mother to child. A third of the world's population is estimated to carry toxoplasmosis, especially women of childbearing age. Infection typically causes mild, flu-like symptoms. However, it may cause serious illness in those with weakened immune systems. Recent research has linked toxoplasmosis with attention deficit hyperactivity disorder, obsessive compulsive disorder, schizophrenia, and suicidal behavior.

"Basically, the subjects are the cats, and we're the rats," I guessed.

"Not exactly. It's the other way around. The cat carries the hidden infection, and the rat suffers the brain damage and behavioral changes. The parasite doesn't appear to care who eats who, as long as the reproductive cycle is complete."

"That can't be the whole story," I protested. "Infected rats can't survive under water, or go for weeks without food. They don't keep moving after their guts are torn out, or their skin is burned off. Infected rats don't come back from the dead and try to eat cats!"

"I know. I know. It's a mutation or something." She shrugged. "I wish we had more answers, but we don't. That's why we have to keep searching. The weirdest thing is that this strain doesn't affect rats. They're carriers, but they don't change. I'd know more if I could dissect a cat."

Chapter Twenty-Three: Ammunition Duty

After lunch, I had ammunition duty with Staci in the Armory. Refilling magazines and counting bullets was the most useful thing Staci could do. Given the Major's new agenda, I guess he wanted to increase production.

Whatever weapons and ammunition local and county law enforcement had after the collapse were stored in the Armory. New Hampshire is also a gun-friendly state, and many refugees arrived with their own weapons caches, which were promptly confiscated. And the Runners brought back whatever they could salvage from abandoned buildings nearby. Our job was to sort a big bucket of loose rounds into ammunition boxes organized by caliber, and to reload empty magazines so the Runners and Watchers were always ready at a moment's notice. Our workstation was the secretary's desk before the collapse.

After the bell, Major Winters and Private Woz ran into the room with their new recruits. The Major counted them as they came in, and ordered them to line up. Officer Cordell stood like a soldier, but the others took more coaching from Woz. The Major screamed at them unintelligibly until they were lined up to his satisfaction. They were panting and coated in sweat from running drills in the auditorium.

The Major counted ten recruits. Officer Cordell was the most eager to play soldier, but he wasn't the first to finish the run. Ahead of him was a tall Irish man with broad shoulders and a soft presence, lumbering like a giant when he ran.

The eleventh man was Mr. Ash, looking dizzy from exhaustion. The Major stepped in his way. "Hit the showers, Tubby. You're off the squad."

"Thank God!" Mr. Ash panted, visibly relieved.

"And tell everyone left in the hall that they're out, too!" The Major walked up and down the line, sizing up the men.

93

Moses strolled in with a relaxed stride. He didn't even break a sweat.

"Nice of you to join us, Cadet! I hope we're not inconveniencing you," the Major barked sarcastically.

"No, suh. Ah take meh time, but ah always get dere soon enough." Moses smiled.

"Get out of here. I don't like your attitude."

"Yes, suh." Moses made a small, almost mocking salute, and strolled out of the room.

The Major turned toward the line. "I do not tolerate slackers in my company. Do you understand?"

The recruits nodded and answered yes, but not to the Major's satisfaction.

"When I ask you a question, you answer 'Yes, Sir' as loud as you can. Do you understand?"

"Yes, Sir!" everyone called back in unison.

"DO YOU UNDERSTAND?"

"YES, SIR!"

"Good," he answered at a normal volume. The Major faced off with the large Irish man. "First place again, Cadet!" The Major beamed. "What's your name?"

"Simon," he replied

"What'd you do before, Simon?"

"Boxing."

"Well, Simon the Boxer, what's your story? You got a score to settle with those meat puppets?"

Simon shook his head no.

"Well, what is it?" the Major pressed.

"I'm just following orders."

The Major paused, and laughed, slapping Simon on the shoulder. "I love this guy! Ready to sacrifice for his fellow man. Ready to obey with honor!"

He paused again, stood in front of the line and yelled, "Attention!" The men tightened their already rigid postures. "When I say your number, you're going to say your name! Do you understand?"

"Yes, Sir!" They all yelled.

"Then you are going to tell us what you did before the world went to Hell! Do you understand?"

"Yes, Sir!"

"Number two!"

"Matt Cordell! Grafton County Sheriff's Deputy, Sir!" Matt yelled.

"I've seen you in action. You're a good Runner."

Matt nodded.

"You got the skills. You got the attitude. Welcome aboard, Matt. Glad to have you. Number three!"

"Kevin Dupre. Dog catcher, Sir!" Kevin was a fit young man, with spiked, blond hair.

"That explains the running speed," commented the Major. "Welcome aboard. Number four!"

"Cody Grimes. Thorton Police, and I'm a Runner." Cody was a mousy-faced man with a dopey, disconnected look.

"You got something to say to me, Cody Grimes?" Asked the Major.

"No."

The Major got in his face. "I don't like the way you're looking at me."

Cody stepped back and looked at his feet, and the major pushed forward. "Did I tell you to break ranks, Number Four?"

"Man, get off of me." Cody pushed the Major back, but the Major quickly yanked his arms behind his back, and put him face-down on the floor. "Oh, I'm on you, Number Four!" The Major put his boot on Cody's face. "I'm all over you, until you learn some respect! This is not some small-town police action anymore, and I am not some glad-handing Sheriff that needs your vote. I am a Major in the United States Armed Forces, and on this squad you will behave with the precision that institution commands. Do you get me?"

"Yeth." His answer was muffled by the Major's boot.

"Yes, what?" he screamed.

"Yeth, Thir!"

"Good man." He released Cody, and turned back to the line. "Number five!"

"Andre Andrew, Sir! I used to hustle, Sir."

"Used to what?" Asked the Major.

"Uh, odd jobs mostly, Sir. I drove a cab, cleaned houses, sold cars. Stuff like that. Sir." Andre was clearly shaken by what happened to Cody. He was putting extra emphasis on his *sirs*.

"I see." The Major scratched his chin. "I've never been able to trust a man with two first names."

Andre visibly tensed.

The Major laughed. "I'm just messing with you! Good man." Andre relaxed. "Number six!"

"Manuel Ramos, Sir. I'm the school coach." Coach Ramos was short and fat, with dark hair and a thick mustache. His fat neck and double chin made him look like he was leaning his head back.

"Welcome aboard. Number seven."

"Joe Weekley. SWAT." Joe was a young guy, tough and confident.

"SWAT! That's what I like to hear!" The Major looked surprised. "Did you drive one of those armored vehicles out front?"

"Um… No, Sir."

"Wait a minute. How have we had a SWAT officer under our roof this whole time, and I've never met you? You're not a Runner, or a Watcher?"

"I was removed from active duty before everything happened."

"For what?"

"Excessive force."

The Major chuckled. "Come on. We both know local cops don't get fired for excessive force. What really happened?"

Joe gulped. "Excessive force… against my wife."

"I see. And is she still with us?"

"No, Sir."

"Excellent! Then there's no problem. So you've got a temper. That's practically an asset these days. Consider yourself reinstated. Welcome aboard." The Major moved on. "Number eight."

"Clifford Whall. High school lacrosse, Sir." It was the guy from the cafeteria who made fun of Staci.

"Seriously, your name is Cliff Wall? Did your mom give birth between a rock and a hard place?" asked the Major. I chuckled to myself.

"No, Sir." Clifford didn't get the joke. "I was born in Thornton."

"You a sophomore?"

"A junior," Clifford answered.

"What position did you play?"

"Attacker."

"Alright then. Welcome aboard." He smiled. "Number nine."

"Theodore Parrish, Sir." He was an older man, with a gray mustache and a receding hairline.

"And?" asked the Major.

"And I'm retired" Theodore answered in an uncooperative tone.

"Retired from what?" The Major smiled smugly.

Theodore paused and took a deep breath before answering. "I was a thief."

The police all looked down the line and gave Theodore a threatening look. Woz began laughing, and grabbed his mouth with both hands to stop himself.

"You'd be surprised how valuable those talents are now," Major said, glaring at Woz. "Welcome aboard. Number Ten."

"Scott Pike, Sir. Student Patrol."

The Major frowned. "Son, how old are you?"

"Fifteen."

"No way!" I blurted out. I didn't mean to, but Scott couldn't be more than a year older than me, maybe two. He definitely wasn't fifteen.

The Major spun around. "Can the peanut gallery shut up?"

Scott made a slashing motion over his throat. I'm not sure if he meant, "Shut up," or "I'll slit your throat if you don't shut up," but the message was clear.

"Yes, Sir," I mumbled.

The Major turned back to Scott. "You're John Pike's son, aren't you?"

"Yes, Sir."

"Your father is a great man, and we all owe him a great debt for his service." He put his hand on Scott's shoulder. "Do you have what it takes to be an effective member of this squad?"

Scott nodded.

"Good man." The Major smiled. "Welcome aboard." He clapped and rubbed his palms together as he walked back to the front. "Alright! We've done hand-to-hand combat, strength training, speed, and endurance. You ten maggots are the very best that this dumpster has to offer, so consider yourselves drafted. I hope you enjoyed today, because we're doing drills every morning until this is a proper kill squad. Do you understand?"

"Yes, Sir," they said.

"I said, DO YOU UNDERSTAND!?"

"YES, SIR!"

"Good. Now, we're spending the rest of the day firearms training. Show of hands. Who has ever fired a handgun?"

All the cops raised their hands, but none as enthusiastically and Matt Cordell. Andre, Coach Ramos, and Theodore also raised their hands.

I raised mine, too.

"What about a long gun? Keep those hands up." The Major continued.

Half the hands went down, leaving only Weekley, Cordell, and Andre, but I kept mine up. The Major looked surprised, and smirked at me.

The cadets were partnered up so each pair had an experienced gunman to train the other. Major Winters picked Simon, Private Woz picked Kevin, Officer Cordell picked Scott, Officer Weekley picked Theodore, and Officer Grimes picked Clifford, leaving Coach Ramos and Andre as partners.

"Attention!" screamed the Major.

The men returned to their rigid postures.

"Trainers! Select your arms! Trainees! Get to the roof! You have thirty seconds, now move!"

Everyone burst into motion as the Major stood beneath the skylight, counting down from thirty.

"Now we know why the Major asked for another kid on ammo duty," joked Staci.

"Why's that?" I asked.

"I'm not exactly good with ladders." She pointed as Coach Ramos and Simon extended a telescoping ladder through the skylight.

Woz yelled, "Move! Move! Move!" as everyone scrambled up. He pointed at me. "You! Grab all the sorted ammo we have, and get up there. Come on! Move!"

I grabbed every box and loaded magazine I could carry.

"I told you." Staci smiled before I climbed up.

Chapter Twenty-Four: The Outside

Icy wind hit me as I reached the roof.

The world had transformed with the weather. Everything was coated in a blanket of snow so bright, it was blinding until my eyes adjusted. The roads had disappeared, because no one was plowing them. The refugee tents, jungle gym, and cars were covered with white. Beyond the fences, it looked like the forest went on forever. With no human activity, the developed world had returned to nature.

There were only a few creepers around. So quiet.

The roof had two levels, with a second ladder set up to get to the auditorium's roof.

In front of the school, the new Thornhaven banner replaced the American flag.

The helicopter was on the first level. It was olive green, and based on the markings, clearly military. From the look of it, the landing had been rough. It had demolished one of the school's turbine vents. The main rotor and landing gear were crushed. It wouldn't fly again, but it got me thinking. At first, I thought I could use the fuel to burn through the back of my locker, but even jet fuel wouldn't melt steel. Then I thought maybe it had a battery. Battery acid is about 30% sulfuric acid, diluted with water. Strong acid would corrode steel.

On the right-hand side, near the engine, I spotted a panel labeled "battery door." While everyone was focused on the Major, I pried it open with my multi-tool. Sure enough, it was a lead-acid battery, just like a car battery, only about twice the size. I loosened the bolts that held it in place, but it was way too heavy for me to move. I'd have to come back at night when it was least crowded and siphon out the fluid.

"We need a target." Major Winters pulled out a bottle of Granite State Vodka. I could tell by the blood that it was Judge Burke's. He finished it and chucked it over the side of the building. "First team to break that gets double rations tomorrow."

Major Winters, Simon, Cordell, Scott, Grimes, and Clifford stayed on the first level for handgun training. Woz, Kevin, Andre, Ramos, Weekley, and Theodore went to the second level for rifle training. Woz and the Major communicated over handheld CB radios, just like what Ellie and I used. I was instructed to go back and forth, and make sure everyone had all the ammo they needed.

Gunfire rang out. After Andre broke the vodka bottle, a favorite target was the "Gun Free Zone" sign on the front gate. By the time they blew that off its bolts, the noise had attracted moving targets.

Maybe it was the cold, or because they were falling apart, but the creepers were slower, dragging through at a crawl. They were more decomposed, and they jabbed their jaws compulsively. Some of them had chewed right through their own cheeks, and I could see their putrid tongue flicking around.

A black bird swooped down from a nearby tree and plucked the left eye right out of an old creeper's head. It grabbed at the bird, trying to catch its own meal, but the bird was too fast.

Woz and Winters used something called "HERD reports" to communicate intelligence on the creepers. HERD stood for "Heads, Equipment, Rate, and Direction," but not necessarily in that order. Heads meant the number of creepers. Equipment for what they were carrying, or identifying clothes. Rate and Direction described their movement. HERD reports were designed to be quick and accurate, with the most important information first.

"One crawler. Northeast. Body armor," or, "Six walkers. Due south. Wedding party," and "Ten lurkers. Due west. Teenagers with backpacks." That sort of thing.

As the creepers inched closer, the cadets shot faster, and less accurately.

"Hey, Kid!" Andre waved me over. I grabbed some ammo out of my book bag for him, but he didn't need it. "Matt tells me you're the one who brought this rifle in. Is that true?" It was the gold engraved Winchester 70 Featherweight we took from Judge Burke's house.

I nodded.

"And the owners, do you know what happened to them?"

I nodded again.

"Are they alive?" I shook my head.

"Damn." He stood the rifle on the ground and looked to the sky. "Do me a favor, don't tell Livia."

"I'm sick of all the secrets around here," I whispered.

"It's not a secret." He took a deep breath. "I just want to tell her myself. They're her parents. She should hear it from me."

I nodded.

I spun around when I heard Woz's signature hysterical laughter. Kevin was heating snow over a fire pit and Woz was dumping it over the side. It exploded in a billow of steam.

"What are you doing?" I asked.

"Ice sculptures." Woz wiped a tear from his eye. "Look."

There were four creepers, three frozen in terrifying poses, and a fourth was soaking wet, clawing at the building. It slowed down, eventually stopped, and fell on its back, the snarl frozen on its face.

Woz and Kevin rolled with laughter before going back to melting the next pot of snow.

"Does that kill them?" I asked.

"No, just slows them down." Woz giggled. "By the time they thaw out, they forget what they were doing, and wander away."

Sheriff Nap climbed onto the roof. "Everybody stop! Hold your fire!" He waved his arms. "You can't do this! You'll bring the whole mob on us!"

I climbed down to the first level.

The Major was taking aim at an elderly woman in the yard. "Calm down, Old Man." He took the shot, dropping the creeper, and looked up from the pistol sites without changing his stance. "We've got more than enough rounds for this herd."

"What about the next one? And the next? You can't waste limited resources! This community has survived by avoiding detection. I'm not going to let you risk that for some target practice!" Sheriff Nap stepped in front of the Major's Beretta. "Are you going to stop, or am I going to have to make you stop?"

"So, the local Sheriff thinks he's got guts." The Major grinned. "Tell me, old man, what makes you so sure I won't put a slug through those guts for insubordination?" He pressed the gun muzzle into Nap's ribs.

The whole roof went silent.

"You think these people will miss you?" said Winters. "What makes you think they won't thank me for the extra rations?" He poked him with the barrel to punctuate his threat. Woz laughed.

Simon pushed the Major's muzzle aside, and stood between the men with his hands raised. "Okay, guys. Enough goofing around. We've had enough practice for one day."

In the yard, more than thirty creepers inched toward Thornhaven.

"They'll forget about this by the time they get here." Winters pulled the trigger and a creeper dropped. The crack echoed for miles. "Okay, men, let's pack it in. Matt and Woz, you're on watch. Everyone else get some rest. I want everyone up at dawn for drills. Then we'll pick teams for yard duty. I'll whip this pudgy crew into a kill squad before you know it."

Chapter Twenty-Five: Battery Acid

That night, as everyone fell asleep, I waited until the lights went off in the security office. Once I knew whoever was monitoring the surveillance cameras was off duty, I snuck into the science lab. I had my own keys, and I needed to borrow some equipment.

Sulfuric acid is extremely corrosive, and can cause terrible chemical burns to exposed skin. I grabbed safety goggles and rubber gloves. Even breathing the vapors can be dangerous, so I grabbed a paper face mask, too.

Then I grabbed a box of baking soda. Acids and bases are opposites in chemistry. Battery acid is pretty strong stuff. Baking soda, or sodium bicarbonate, is a common base compound that's perfect to quickly neutralize a strong acid, in case of a spill.

Finally, I grabbed an empty spray bottle and a pipette, which is like a small turkey baster. Both were made of polyethylene plastic, which is resistant to strong acids.

Next, I had to collect the battery acid. The halls were dark, and the roof was even darker, so I brought Ellie's flashlight with me. I climbed the ladder in the Armory and poked my head up through the skylight to see who was on watch duty.

It was Coach Ramos. I could make out the shape of his fat belly in the glow of his campfire.

I took a rock and chucked it over the top of the helicopter into the yard below. *Ping!* The sound was clear and loud. I must have hit a pole in the playground. It definitely got his attention.

Ramos perked up, staring into the dark night. He groaned as he climbed to his feet, readied his rifle, and walked to the edge of the roof to investigate.

That was my chance. With his back to me, I slinked across the roof until I was safely behind the helicopter, where I could work.

I opened the battery door and brushed all the dirt and debris off the top of the battery with a rag and some melted snow. Using the pliers on my multi-tool, I removed the positive and negative terminals so the battery was disconnected, then I pried the plastic cover off the top of the battery, revealing the cells inside.

It was a 24-volt battery, so it had twelve cells. A typical car battery had twelve volts and only six cells, but the concept was the same. Each cell was sealed with a circular port, which I removed by twisting a quarter turn and lifting out.

Now I could see the fluid levels in each individual cell, and by dipping the pipette through the port openings, I was able to suck out the fluid and deposit it in the spray bottle. The battery acid was thick like oil, with a slight yellow color. I extracted just enough to fill a third of the spray bottle, about three hundred milliliters. Then I sealed the ports, closed the cover, and got the heck out of there.

Back at the lab, I had space and equipment to work. Now, battery acid is about 30% sulfuric acid, and 70% water. Most people would think I should concentrate the acid by cooking off the water over a Bunsen burner, but sulfuric acid is different than most other strong acids. It needs water to react with iron, and steel is an alloy of iron and carbon. What I needed was a solution of about 10% sulfuric acid, and 90% water. Diluted sulfuric acid would dissolve the iron in the steel, producing hydrogen gas, salt, and heat.

Ms. Lessard didn't teach this stuff in eighth grade science class. I learned it being the son of a scientist, and visiting Dad in his lab. Dad loved explaining things when he was working, explaining the chemistry, explaining the safety procedures. Even dead, he was still helping me.

I filled the spray bottle with water, which bubbled in the acid. In fact, the bottom of the bottle began to bevel as it softened from the heat, and I worried it might burst, but it cooled after the solution settled. That was dangerous. I should have done the mixing in a glass container, I realized.

I found some steel washers in the equipment cabinet and placed them in a glass petri dish. Using the pipette, I drew out some of the diluted acid and dripped it on them until they were submerged. Sure enough, they foamed and sizzled as they dissolved in the acid. I was ready.

I went to the locker room and emptied everything out of my locker. I put on all the safety gear and sprayed the acid on the back panel. I only sprayed once at first, and then stood back to observe. Nothing happened. I leaned in, and the spritz was bubbling slightly. I sprayed three more times, and the acid accumulated and dripped down the panel, but there was no significant reaction.

Suddenly, the paint began to melt away, revealing the raw steal underneath, and immediately the acid began to sizzle and billow milky white vapors. The paint must have been some kind of protective coating. I stood back.

I sprayed more acid periodically to keep the reaction going. Within minutes, it had eaten a hole through the steel panel, and I could see the inside of the locker on the other side. I sprayed more around the edges of the hole, to widen it.

Once the hole was large enough, I sprinkled the baking soda to neutralize the acid. I coated the entire area until all the bubbling stopped, and then I rinsed out the whole locker with water and paper towels from the restroom. I neutralized the acid in the spray bottle with baking soda before flushing it all down the toilet.

When it was finished, the hole looked large enough for me to squeeze through. I looked inside the broken locker and found a copy of *The Alchemist* by Paulo Coelho. The library card on the inside cover said it hadn't been checked out since 2003.

I hid my gear bag in the secret compartment. I stashed all the survival gear I had left, the trauma kit, and any nonperishable food they served, but what I really needed was a weapon. I kept Ellie's book bag to carry my zPad and everyday items.

I needed to cover the hole, though. So I unfolded Ellie's roadmap and taped it inside the locker. It worked perfectly. From the outside, my locker looked just like any other.

I noticed that Lochshire was circled on her map, as though she'd intended to go there. That was strange.

Chapter Twenty-Six: The Library Mutiny

When I snuck back under my covers, Stinky was there waiting for me, just like he did in Lochshire.

"Stinky, you have to be more careful now," I whispered. He nuzzled under my chin.

"It's only a matter of time before they find him," said Holland from the dark.

"Do you ever sleep?"

"Undead monsters that want to eat us, right on the other side of that door. I'm amazed any of you can sleep."

"So, you just sit awake all night?" I asked.

"Sometimes I pass out. Sometimes I wander the halls."

"What's it like at night?"

"Quiet. The Watchers are on the roof, but there's almost no one in the halls. Sometimes, people are awake upstairs, but they're so obsessed with the outside they don't bother patrolling the inside anymore."

"Don't people steal food?"

"The pantry is locked, and the Armory, and the boiler room. Everything else is open."

"The library?" I asked.

"Open. I go there all the time."

I got out of bed, put on my shoes, and grabbed Ellie's book bag. "I gotta get something." Stinky meowed. I motioned to him. "You can come, but keep quiet." Stinky leapt after me and we left.

"I'm coming, too!" Holland ran after us, his heavy feet clomping loudly.

"Fine, but keep it down," I whispered.

The library was open just like Holland had said, and I went straight to the Local Authors section and grabbed *The Porcupine Freedom Scouts Survival Guide* by Rich Hartwell. A rubber stamp on the spine read "Property of Thornton Middle School," but I checked the journal pages in the back and my handwritten notes were there. I threw it in the book bag and started to leave when I saw another book. *Psychoclass A* by Joy Hartwell. *Mom!* I read the dedication.

> *"Dedicated to my unborn stranger. May you find this land as strange as I do."*

I flipped through it, but it wasn't about aliens. It was about psychology. I skimmed through the first chapter.

> *"The Beast in the Brain – There is little doubt that we live in an age of aggression, but we cannot heal our world until we acknowledge why it is sick. Studies linking childhood trauma to violence as adults have been widely accepted by the scientific consensus, but the data is rarely made available to the public. This is a detrimental oversight by our society. Once you grok it..."*

Grok? I'd never heard the word before.

> *"Once you grok it, you will never see the world, or even yourself, the same way again. There is a staggering body of evidence that the true root of human violence, criminality, tyranny, and many other dysfunctions, can be traced to child abuse. Physical, sexual, verbal, and emotional abuse are all shamefully common, and all cause physical changes in the developing brain, which are readily visible in scans of adults. The severity of this early damage can be broadly categorized into five psychoclasses, which are the prime determinant of adult aggression. We are not born broken. We are damaged by our experience as children. Let's remedy that."*

I flipped to some glossy pages in the middle, graphs showing the relationship between child abuse and alcoholism, domestic violence, intelligence, life span, cancer, and even memory loss.

Mom wasn't a pediatrician, she was a child psychologist!

"Something must be done!" Someone pounded down on a table somewhere in the library.

Holland and I exchanged panicked looks and parted the books on the shelf in front of us to peek through. It was Sheriff Nap, standing, with his fist on the table. Ms. Lessard, Miss Styx, and Mr. Ash were seated around him.

"What if he's right?" pleaded Ms. Lessard. "We can't stay trapped in here forever. What if clearing the yard is the only way to…"

"It doesn't matter if he's right!" interrupted Miss Styx. "He has no respect for the democratic process. We have to discuss it, consider alternatives, and come to a consensus. He can't just march around pretending to be king."

Mr. Ash crossed his arms over his chest, resting them on his belly. "At least he gets things done. If it weren't for the zip lines those boys set up, we wouldn't even be having this discussion. We wouldn't have electricity. We wouldn't have food. They deserve a little credit."

"He's a loose cannon. Sooner or later, he's going to get people killed," Sheriff Nap yelled. "People, he shoved a gun to my neck and threatened to kill me!"

Wasn't it in his ribs? I thought.

"It's going to upset a lot of people if we let him kill everyone in the yard without a vote," added Miss Styx.

"We have to stop him," insisted Sheriff Nap.

"Yeah, how?" asked Mr. Ash.

"We stand up to him. Confront him," Nap continued. "He's a bully. You don't back down from bullies or they walk all over you."

"You're talking about mutiny," said Ms. Lessard.

"I'm saying local decisions need to be made by local people. If he wants to coordinate a rescue with the Capitol, that's fine, but

Thornhaven is ours. Those people are our friends and family. We can't let him just execute them before we know if a cure is possible."

Miss Styx nodded. "Makes sense to me. He doesn't know us. He doesn't know the effect it will have on the community."

"For the record," added Ms. Lessard, "the chance of a cure isn't looking very good. Even if I could purge the infection, the brain damage is so severe that they'd never be themselves again. Their bodies are rotting."

Nap plopped in his seat. "Makes no difference. Medical decisions belong to the next of kin, not some officious bureaucrat in the Capitol, and certainly not some jackboot army officer still high on the adrenaline of his first combat mission."

"Let's say we did confront him," said Mr. Ash. "How would we do it? He's got a small army now."

"He's got recruits, but not loyalty," Nap countered. "Some of them will side with us, and if we make a significant show of force, he'll have to back down."

"Oh no!" Miss Styx protested. "An armed standoff is a terrible idea! Once the community is unified against the idea, I'm sure he'll listen to reason."

"Tell that to Officer Pike," quipped Nap under his breath.

"What's that supposed to mean?" asked Mr. Ash.

"It means he's been awfully vague about what happened that night," said Nap.

"Let's not go crazy with speculation," interrupted Ms. Lessard.

The Sheriff insisted, "I'm not speculating! I think he..."

Thump. A book hit the floor. Holland had pushed the books apart to get a better view, and accidentally knocked a paperback off the other side. It didn't make much noise, but in the dead of night, it was unmistakable.

"What was that?" interrupted Miss Styx.

"Who's there?" called Mr. Ash.

I covered Holland's mouth and pulled him away. Sheriff Nap and Ms. Lessard inched toward us. Nap picked up the book, and started coming around the shelf.

110

The sound of falling pencils echoed on the other side of the room, diverting everyone's attention.

It was Stinky, knocking things off the librarian's desk. He meowed at them when they saw him.

They all had a look of relief, except Ms. Lessard, who had a look of ambition. "A cat!" she exclaimed, moving toward him.

Stinky jumped off the desk, but she grabbed him.

"Be careful!" screamed Miss Styx. "It might be infected!"

Holland opened the library door and tried to push me out, but I shoved back. "No! We can't leave him with her," I whispered.

Stinky hissed, dug his claws into Ms. Lessard's face, and bit her upper lip. She screamed and threw him on the floor.

In a flash, Stinky disappeared between the bookshelves, darted between my legs, into the hall, and out of sight. Holland and I followed him out before they saw us.

"You're an experiment."

The next morning, Stinky was gone. Wherever he went, he was fending for himself. Holland was still awake, reading *Psychoclass A*.

"What are you talking about?" I asked.

"It's all in the book," he said. "Child abuse leaves scar tissue in your brain. All the aggressive parts get bigger, and all the rational parts get smaller. These scientists scanned people's brains looking for test subjects from all five brain types, but they couldn't find anyone in Psychoclass A—someone with absolutely no scar tissue. So, the scientists got together and devised an experiment to raise their own test subjects from birth. No punitive discipline, no hierarchical instruction, and no compulsory schooling. Just cruelty-free, home-grown, free-range human. Joy Hartwell, that's your mom right? That makes you part of Psychoclass A."

"Give me that!" I snatched the book from him. "You can't just take other people's stuff without asking."

"Whatever. I was almost finished, anyway."

"Crazy!" Staci was also awake, listening to us. "So Egghead has some kind of super brain? Freak show!"

We argued a bit more, but when the first bell rang, it was time for the morning routine.

After washing and eating, we went to the Armory to check the day's work detail. There was commotion near the door. Miss Styx was going down the list with a red pen, writing, "Cancelled, cancelled, cancelled," over the first period assignments. A crowd of faculty and other townspeople seemed ready to confront the Major, and any loyal recruits.

Tension was in the air, ready to snap as soon as the Major's kill squad finished their morning drills, but where there was conflict, I saw opportunity. Amid the commotion, no one was left upstairs. I grabbed Holland, and headed to find Officer Pike's room.

We ran up the steps, and bumped right into Scott. "Hartwell! Where the heck are you going? Kids aren't allowed up here. I'm gonna write you up for this."

"No, you're not!" I insisted. "This is bigger than hall passes and Student Patrol. Scott, you deserve the truth."

"What truth?"

"That's what we're going to find out. Last night, we heard Sheriff Nap talking to some faculty about your dad." I looked to Holland and he nodded to back me up. "That's part of what the demonstration at the Armory is about. We're going to your dad's room to figure out what happened to him. You should come with us."

Scott rolled his eyes. "Not this again. I told you, my dad is delivering ballots to the Capitol, just like the Major said. He probably just got caught in the snow." He considered carefully. "I better go with you and make sure you don't steal anything, and when you see that I'm right, you'll owe me half your rations for a week."

"Deal!" I said.

It was a good thing he came, because Scott knew where Pike's room was. It was small and looked like it served as a supply room before the collapse. There were paint buckets in the school colors, a shelf of cleaning supplies, stacks of folding tables and chairs, and bins of sports equipment. There was a cot, like the ones in the auditorium, although the blanket was nicer. His clothes hung on a rolling garment rack from the theater department.

"Why would they keep this room empty if he wasn't coming back?" Scott asked.

"To maintain the lie," answered Holland.

"If the Major is in contact with the Capitol, why wouldn't he count the votes himself and radio it in?" I asked.

"Because Thornhaven is the most northern safe zone," answered Scott. "Dad has to pick up the ballots from Concord, Manchester, Boston, and everywhere else along the way."

I eyed him skeptically. Under the cot was a small toiletries bag. "If he went on this long mission, why didn't he take his toothbrush?"

Scott had no answer.

"Guys!" called Holland. "Check this out. It's weird." In the back of the room was a workstation. The area was peppered with handwritten notes from Pike's memo pad, mostly about conversations he'd overheard about Winters. The main work area had a map of the East Coast. There were red correction pen markings of concentric circles around Thornton. Handwritten in the middle of the Atlantic Ocean was, "The Capitol – Thornton: 385nmi | Manchester – Thornton: 59nmi | UH – 72: 370nmi"

"See!" Scott beamed. "He was plotting his course to the Capitol."

"What's nmi?" I asked.

"Nautical Miles," Holland answered. Scott and I looked at him, puzzled. "What? My dad was a pilot."

"Why would he convert to nautical miles when the map is already in miles?" I asked.

"Maybe he wanted to take the helicopter?" said Scott.

"No," I rebutted. "It's in no condition to fly. Besides, what is UH and Seventy-two?"

"Is there a Highway Seventy-two?" Scott asked. "Maybe he found a shorter route."

"That doesn't make sense," I insisted. "A highway can't be shorter than a straight line."

"Guys, look!" Holland pulled a blue booklet out of the waste basket.

The cover read, "UH-72 Lakota Flight Manual."

"It's the helicopter!" we all said in unison.

"I bet..." Holland flipped through it. "Yeah! Three hundred and seventy nautical miles is the range of the helicopter. Look, Pike circled it the same red ink." He held the page out to us. "But that doesn't make sense. The Capitol is too far away. Even on a full tank, this helicopter can't get here from there.

Scott had a dark look on his face. "It makes perfect sense if they're not from the Capitol."

"Whoa!" I exclaimed. "I remember who Winters is!" I grabbed the zPad out of my book bag and booted it up. "I knew he was familiar as soon as I saw him, but I couldn't remember. Look at this video I downloaded right after the outbreak."

I played the video. It was at the FEMA camp in Manchester, only a few months ago, but Winters looked years younger as he stared into the camera, panicked, and confused. "We held the wall! They came from inside the green zone. How'd they get in there? We held the wall!"

It was before they knew about the hidden infection.

Scott fumed. "I think it's time we talked to whoever's on the other end of the Major's radio." He charged out of the room.

Chapter Twenty-Eight: Undelete

We chased Scott to the Major's office, but it was locked. The key was on the Major's rabbit foot keyring.

"I have the AV club keys in my locker," said Holland. Before the collapse, the security office doubled as the AV room. It was the only office with enough screens to monitor all the video feeds so it used to be Pike's office, too. "There's no way he changed the locks. There's no locksmith."

"I got the key!" Scott busted open the door with a SWAT raid-style boot to the knob.

The Major's office was full of computers, most of which were no longer used. He kept the surveillance system active, allegedly for security, but four of the five cameras were pointed inside. One was pointed at the playground behind the school, the auditorium, the cafeteria, and the main hall, where we could see people gathered outside the Armory, and one in the Armory, where the argument between Winters and Nap was escalating.

Scott went to the Major's desk and grabbed a steel briefcase with rounded corners and black-and-yellow letters that read, "Wideband Global SatCom." It was a satellite communications system used by the military. Even if every radio tower in the world was destroyed, it should work as long as the military satellites were still in orbit. Scott struggled to pry it open before realizing it had a combination lock.

"Whoa! Look at that," Holland pointed to the outside camera monitor where a herd of over a hundred wandered through holes in the fence. They were slow, but the herd was massive.

"The gunfire yesterday must have drawn them," I said.

"It's a good thing they heard the morning bell," said Holland. "Look. They're still lining up." As the creepers approached, they joined the others lining up for the morning bell.

Scott wedged a letter opener under the SatCom case's locking mechanism. He got frustrated and lifted the case over his head and slammed it on the desk. The handle broke clean off and was still in his hand. The case bounced off the desk, and tumbled onto the floor.

"An empty case!" screamed Scott, slamming his fists on the desk.

Holland and I exchanged knowing glances. No radio meant no Capitol. No Capitol meant no votes. No votes meant no mission. So, what happened to Pike?

"Are these videos saved somewhere?" I asked Holland, moving toward the security computer.

"I don't know," he answered. "Why?"

"I'm way ahead of you," interrupted Scott as he opened the desk file drawer and sifted through a stack of memory cartridges. He grabbed one and went to the surveillance computer. "This is the day Dad left."

"How do you know about that?" Holland asked.

"Where do you think I spent Take Your Child to Work Day?" Scott handed the cartridge to Holland. "Load it."

Holland took it and swiveled into the workstation. The last hours of the recording, including the night Pike left, were deleted.

"Dammit!" Scott pounded his fists.

"Not so fast!" said Holland. "The AV Club has an undelete program." He rolled over to the AV computer and booted it up. He reached toward Scott at the security computer. "Hand it over." Scott ejected the cartridge and tossed it to Holland.

"What's an undelete program?" I asked.

Holland shoved the cartridge into the reader and started the program. "Most things aren't as deleted as you think they are. On any system using a file allocation table, deletion doesn't erase data. It just marks the data fields as free space, so it looks deleted in the operating system."

He saw our confusion, and reconsidered his answer. "When you delete files, the computer doesn't wipe the memory, it just tags it as open space. It looks empty, but it's not. As long as nothing gets recorded over them, the files can be recovered. You just need a way to read the raw data. That's what an undelete program does."

His fingers flew over the keyboard and the screen flashed as the program reassembled the scattered blocks of deleted files.

Scott stood behind him, looked at me, and mouthed, "Niles?" pointing at Holland.

I shrugged.

"Why do you even have that program?" Scott asked.

"Teachers used to confiscate our recording equipment. They'd have to eventually give it back, but if they didn't like the footage, they'd delete it." He turned and pointed his finger in the air. "You can't stop the signal." He kept typing. "It isn't foolproof. Solid state drives, and some flash drives wipe the free space. But this is just an old SD card. If you want to securely delete stuff, you've got to use a file shredder. I've got that program on here, too. What that does is rewrite the deleted file space with random, meaningless data. That way, the actual data is overwritten permanently."

"We don't care about shredding stuff." Scott sounded frustrated. "We just want to see the video."

"All done." Holland pushed play. "Take a look."

* * *

It was the feed from the outside camera at night, before the snow. There were no creepers in the shot, but it was dark, and quiet.

Matt Cordell walked into the shot, surveying the area, and motioned for someone off-screen to follow him.

John Pike appeared. "What are we doing out here? It's not safe."

"I wanted to talk somewhere I knew the Major wasn't listening." Cordell looked over Pike's shoulder, into the camera. "I'm hearing rumors about the things you've been saying."

"They're not rumors!" Pike boomed.

"Shh!" Cordell put his finger to his lips. "Keep it down. There's no telling what else is out here."

"I'm telling you, the Major is not who he says he is!"

"Alright, alright. Calm down. I'm listening." Cordell put his hand on his gun and glanced around. "I get it. We townspeople gotta stick together. I don't like some Fed barking orders at me, either."

"I'll bet he stole that uniform, and the helicopter."

"John, you sound like a conspiracy theorist."

"It's not a theory!" Pike shouted.

"Okay, okay. I believe you, but it doesn't matter. If we do this, we go all the way. I gotta know... do you have proof he isn't who he says he is?"

Pike nodded eagerly. "It's up in my room right now."

"And you can show me?"

"Yes."

"Show everyone?"

"Yes!"

"That's all I need to hear." Cordell gave a military salute to the camera.

As Pike turned, a gunshot rang out. There was an explosion under Pike's shoulder. He fell to his knees and slumped forward, gasping for air, as blood pooled beneath him.

The salute had been a signal.

In the background was the familiar sound of Woz's hysterical laughter.

* * *

"Stop the tape." I nudged Holland. "We don't need to see this." I turned to Scott. "I'm so sorry."

Scott's nostrils flared. His jaw clenched, and his brow tightened. "I'll kill him!" His boot smashed glass as he pulled a fire ax from its case. The fire alarm sounded, and he ran out.

"Scott, wait!" I started chasing him, but Holland pulled me back.

"Max, look!" He pointed to the outside live feed. The rows of creepers charged forward, pressing against the building. The fire alarm had rallied the herd.

Chapter Twenty-Nine: Over the Edge

I couldn't look away from the screen. Every creeper in the yard turned and charged toward the school, biting and scratching the walls. They climbed and trampled over each other. The herd was so thick they blacked out the screen. No sky, no yard, no trees, no snow. Just hundreds of frostbitten corpses. They ripped down the camera, and the feed went blank.

On the inside cameras, people were panicking, running in every direction. Winters and Nap climbed out on the roof.

Holland and I heard a scream and ran to the stairs. Staci was downstairs in the main hall, covering her eyes with her hands. We ran down, but she couldn't speak. She just pointed. At the far end of the hall, the chains holding the exit door were pulled tight. The wood wedged in the handles bounced as the gap between the double doors filled with crooked, pale fingers.

A bloody palm slapped the small window in the science wing door, just a few yards from us.

They were inside.

Staci screamed louder, and the gnarled, gray face of Office Pike peered through the window. The bloody palm tightened into a fist and began pounding.

"Shut up!" screamed Holland, but Staci only sobbed more. He shook her by the shoulders. "Shut up! Shut up! Shut up!" She swallowed hard and held it in, wide-eyed.

Pike was joined by more rotting comrades. The door rattled and threatened to bust. They would break through if we didn't do something.

"Holland, help!" I yelled.

He stared at the mashing of hands and faces in the window.

"Holland!"

He jumped.

We broke open the trophy case and grabbed the two largest awards. We tried to wedge the door shut, but the cheap plastic trophies came apart in our hands. I wasn't expecting that.

The window shattered, showering me with broken glass, and Pike pushed its arm through the crack up to its shoulder.

Its cold fingers wrapped around the strap of my book bag. I pounded on its arm and pulled, but couldn't escape.

The window was too small for Pike to get its arm and its face through at the same time, so it tried to drag me back.

Holland grabbed me around the waist and pulled.

More gray hands came through, grabbing at my shoulder, my arm, and a clump of my hair.

I planted a foot against the door as we yanked back, and fingers slipped off me. I belted out a savage scream as a creeper tore off my ear in a fist full of hair and scalp. Blood poured down my neck, and the creeper shoved my ear in its mouth.

Pike held tight, but I was too stunned to pull away. I could barely hear Holland yelling, because everything sounded underwater, and far away in my blood-drenched ear.

The ax came down with a clap and severed Pike's arm at the shoulder, sending me, Holland, and the arm sprawling to the floor. I felt dizzy and weak.

A second strike hit Pike in the forehead, and the undead officer went down. Scott stood over us with the fire ax over his shoulder, like a lumberjack. He pulled me up, and pried the cold dead hand off of me.

"Scott, your dad," I squeaked.

"I know. You told me the truth. I won't forget that." He looked around. "Niles, I mean Holland, whatever, give me a hand." I slumped against the wall as they shoved the entire trophy case in front of the door. It was mostly glass, but the steel frame had weight.

"Holland, you and Staci go around and get everyone in the library," Scott ordered. "That'll buy us some time. It's the safest place."

"I can't, I can't, I..." Staci was still hysterical.

Scott grabbed her by the shoulders. "Listen to me, and listen good! You don't get to be a little kid anymore. So grow up right now, or you're gonna end up geek bait."

She swallowed hard and nodded.

"Good. You and Holland, go."

"What now?" I asked.

"You and me are going to go rally the troops," he answered.

We went to the Armory where the Major's recruits were gearing up to push the creepers back. Winters and Nap were still on the roof with the protesters. I climbed up with Scott's help.

Everyone was split into factions behind the authority figure they supported. Should the camp be under local control or military rule? But the argument went beyond that. Winters and Nap were screaming about rations, schedules, work details, search patterns, salvage priorities, weapons, and every dispute they'd had since Winters arrived. They screamed like wild dogs barking, even over the fire alarm.

Nap threw the first punch, connecting with Winters' jaw. Winters spit hot, red blood in the white snow, but it didn't faze him.

He smiled, and planted his fist in Nap's face, knocking him on his back. He pounced on him, grabbing his chin, and pushing his head in the snow. He planted surgically precise, piston-like blows to Nap's eye.

Nap flailed his arms to block the blows with no success. His screams were muffled by the blood in his mouth.

"You're killing him!" screamed Mrs. Mills.

Simon and Andre grabbed Winters and pulled him off Nap. Winters tried to wrestle them both, but they dragged him away. Nap climbed to his feet, bloody and swollen.

Winters fired his Beretta into the air, and everyone scattered. "You ungrateful parasites!" he roared. "This camp would be dead without me! No food! No safety! All I'm asking for is a little respect from you cowards, a little obedience!" He swept the muzzle across the crowd, and everyone ducked, except for Nap. "Without me, you have no hope of rescue! No contact with the Capitol!"

"Liar!" Scott cried out. "There's no rescue, no radio!" He pointed the ax at Winters and looked to the crowd. "This guy's not even from the Capitol. He's from the Manchester FEMA camp, and went AWOL when the geeks took the place. He's got you all played!"

I showed Pike's notes and the flight manual to Nap. "Look. Even on a full tank, his helicopter can't get here from the Capitol."

Everyone looked to Winters for an explanation, except Matt and Woz.

Winters held his grin. "Baseless accusations. All military equipment outperforms the factory specs. Why would you believe this kid, anyway?"

"I'm Scott Pike. You killed my father when he figured out your game, and I have the video to prove it."

Winters tightened his brow, his eyes darkened and his grin cracked. "Your father was a dim-witted, pork-bellied slob who couldn't win a game of solitaire if he cheated. He was a drain on our resources. If this community had the slightest clue what was good for them, they'd thank me for putting him out of his fat, stupid, lazy existence."

Scott screamed and charged Winters with the ax, but it wasn't raised for a strike. Scott hooked the ax head behind Winters' leg, slammed him with his shoulder, and pushed Winters off the roof.

We ran to the edge and looked over. Winters was in a snowbank pulling his knee to his chest and wincing in pain. The creepers surrounded him, but he fired enough rounds to clear a path. He limped away as about a dozen creepers followed him.

Woz reached for his weapon, but Sheriff Nap had a handgun on him first. Nap's face was covered in blood and his left eye was swollen shut. "Not so fast, Helicopter Boy." He drew a second handgun on Matt. "Seems to me that you thugs ought to be getting after your boy."

"What, why me?" Matt protested.

"You think I haven't been watching you, Matt? A badge heavy like you, eager to please the military brass." He shook the muzzle toward the zip line.

Woz backed away, but the Sheriff stopped him. "Stop! I think you both better drop your weapons before you go."

Matt dropped his pistol in the snow, and Woz removed his rifle and combat knife.

"You got it all wrong!" Matt insisted. "This is just a misunderstanding."

"I saw what you did!" yelled Scott. "You helped them kill my dad!"

Matt looked defeated and fell to his knees. "Come on, Sheriff. Haven't I saved your tail my fair share? You can't send me out there. You gotta let me stay!"

"Consider this your official termination from the Grafton County Sheriff's Department." The Sheriff turned to Scott. "Son, why don't you check these boys, for good measure?"

Scott patted them down and took the radio off Woz's belt.

"What's it say on it?" asked the Sheriff.

"Property of Rich Hartwell," read Scott.

"Max, that's your dad, isn't it?" asked the Sheriff.

I nodded.

"Scott, you better give that to Max," said the Sheriff.

Winters still had the other radio, so it was useless until I found another one, but it was Dad's. That was everything.

The Sheriff motioned the two men toward the zip line with his pistols. Matt and Woz zipped down to the BEARCAT in the street as Winters crossed the yard. The Sheriff holstered his guns and took Andre's rifle, watching them through the scope, his finger on the trigger.

The three of them fought off the dead with their fists. I'd never seen anything like it. Winters limped into the woods with his arms over their shoulders, and they were gone.

"Why'd you let them go?" Scott asked.

The Sheriff turned to him with his good eye. "The world's a lot smaller now." He stared into the woods. "Sending them out there is worse than any punishment we could have cooked up. Who knows... if they learn a little humility out there, we may see them again. Bring them back into the fold." He put his arm around Scott. "Those men owe you a great debt, Son. If we killed them, they'd never pay it back."

Scott nodded. I think he would have rather chopped them into pieces and fed them to the creepers, but he seemed to understand.

"Guys," I interrupted. "The creepers are still getting in."

The Sheriff straightened up and handed the rifle back to Andre. "I think it's time we cleared the yard, and took back the barricades."

Chapter Thirty: The Day of the Barricades

We climbed down through the skylight and found chaos. The townspeople, once protesting the Kill Squad, were cowering behind them. The cadets: Dupre, Weekley, Parrish, Grimes, and Ramos, were armed and dressed in riot gear, but clueless without orders. Cliff Whall, on the other hand, was hiding under a desk, sobbing.

Officer Weekley pressed his back against the Armory door, resisting the creepers on the other side. "What should we do? Where's the Major?"

"Winters has been decommissioned," barked Sheriff Nap. "You work for me now. I have only one rule. Everyone fights. No one quits. You do your job, or I'll kill you myself!"

Weekley nodded.

"Weekley, you're SWAT so you're my spearhead. Grimes and Dupre," the Sheriff pointed, "grab riot shields, and one for Weekley. Go!"

Grames and Dupre geared up.

"Coach, I'm going to need your swinging arm." He slapped Ramos on the back. "You too, Big Guy." He pointed at Simon. "And you, Parrish. You three grab blades, or blunt-force weapons."

Everyone was ready.

"Shields, you're my frontline. You hold them back, and you do not break ranks. You get me?"

"Yes, Sir," they answered.

"Strikers, you back them up, and swing over their heads. Keep your guns holstered, except as a last resort. You get me?"

"Yes, Sir!"

"Andre, grab your rifle. You're with me, in the back. You only fire when something goes wrong. You keep quiet and save ammo. We have to avoid crowding."

Andre nodded.

"Everyone else, lock yourselves in the Principal's Office, just in case. This is going to get ugly."

Sheriff Nap's strategy was ingenious. The Kill Squad pushed into the main hall with the Shields forming a half circle in front of the Armory door, and the Strikes smashing any creeper that got close.

They cleared enough of the hall to reinforce the front entrance, but the creepers were pouring in through the science wing. They must have forced open the outside door at the other end. The Kill Squad pressed toward the science wing door, but crowding was inevitable.

Officer Weekley screamed and fell on his back. It was Aiyana Jones. She was so small she slipped under his guard, and took a big chomp out of his leg. The creepers reached through the opening in the shield wall and dragged Weekley under the herd. His screams echoed and then gurgled silent as he was devoured. They were down to two shields.

"Fall back!" screamed the Sheriff, firing into the herd. Andre opened fire and they retreated to the next internal fence. Sheriff Nap pulled the fence segment closed, and waved them on. "Move! Move! Move!"

Once it was clear, Nap and I ran to the AV room where he watched the security screens and gave orders over the PA system. The Kill Squad worked in a steady rhythm, transforming the hall into a gauntlet of systematic slaughter.

One Shield, one Striker, and one Shooter were stationed at each internal fence to lure the creepers into caged sections a few at a time and split the herd. Let some in, close them off, smash some skulls, and retreat to the next section. It was gruesome, and efficient.

Any hesitation or exhaustion was considered an unnecessary risk. If any Striker faced a creeper they recognized, especially someone close to them, or they felt fatigued, they switched with the Shield or the Shooter until they'd composed themselves. It was a slow but steady process, one that became monotonous as bodies piled up, a hundred at least.

By noon, all the active creepers in the science wing were cleared. Once the doors were reinforced, they gathered for lunch before going into the yard.

Nurse Mills insisted on treating our injuries.

Nap's face was so swollen it was difficult to assess the damage. She cleaned the blood, applied ice packs, and fed him ibuprofen to reduce the swelling.

My ear was gone except for my earlobe and a bit of cartilage. I could still hear, but everything was muffled. Mrs. Mills shaved my head so she could clean and stitch the wound, and covered it with gauze and a bandage wrapped around my head.

By the end of lunch, Sheriff Nap's swelling went down enough that she could gently open his eyelids. She flushed it with saline solution and gave him an eye exam. The white of the eye was red, and the pupil was tight as a pin prick. "You have a ruptured blood vessel in your eye," she told him. "Possibly traumatic iris inflammation or intracranial bleeding. You've also fractured your orbital socket."

She was unequipped to treat injuries like these. All she could do was give him pain meds and bandage the eye to prevent further injury. Time would tell if he retained vision in that eye.

After lunch, the Kill Squad spread out in the yard. I joined Nap on the roof to cover them with a rifle while he coordinated using police radios. They killed quietly, using minimal ammo. I didn't need to fire a single shot.

They had cleared most of the yard by nightfall, erected the rear fences, closed the front gates, and took back the barricades. The yard was closed. Making it safe, and reoccupying the refugee tents would wait until morning.

Andre volunteered to take watch and everyone else turned in for much needed rest.

Chapter Thirty-One: Seven Simple Rules

I never saw what they did with the bodies. I assume they threw them in the furnace. The next morning, Moses mopped up the blood. It was the only evidence of the brutality that had taken place the day before.

Nap gave the morning announcements instead of the Major, but he didn't say anything about Officer Pike.

*　*　*

> *Good morning, Thornhaven. You may be surprised to hear my voice this morning. A lot has changed in the last twenty-four hours, and there's going to be more changes in the coming weeks, but don't lose heart. One day, we will look back upon The Day of the Barricades as a new dawn in our survival and prosperity.*
>
> *It would be an injustice not to begin with the names of the brave heroes who gave their lives so we might live. Companion Steven Winters, Companion Freddy Wozzeck, and Companion Matt Cordell are no longer with us, but they will not be remembered as Unfortunates. We will remember them as Martyrs of Thornhaven. We will honor their service and sacrifice by carrying on, and not squandering the gift they have given us.*
>
> *We've lost contact with the Capitol, but that's no reason to lose hope. Our independence is an opportunity to show what we're made of when we govern ourselves. We're going to make Thornhaven a hamlet that survivors will flock to, and the numbers will make us stronger. When rescue comes, we won't flee*

our home in desperation. We will be seen as a model and an inspiration to communities everywhere.

If everyone contributes all they can, everyone will receive all they need, so long as we live by seven simple rules.

First, we do not kill the living.

Second, we do not forget the dead.

Third, everyone eats. No more bonus rations. No more secret stashes, or barter. No more going hungry while your Companions eat. We feast or famine together.

Number four, everyone who works gets a vote. I don't care how old you are, or what job you do. Everyone who contributes gets a say in all important decisions facing the community.

Number five, everyone is always on watch. We can no longer entrust our safety to a small team of watchmen. The price of security is eternal vigilance. That means no sleeping during any scheduled shift of any job. It means every able-bodied Companion—man, woman, or child—must receive training and perform guard duty. And it means we do not drink alcohol, or do anything that dulls the senses. Everyone must be ready for crisis at all times.

Rule number six. Three strikes and you're out. We have no use for money so we can't issue fines. We don't have the resources to hold jury trials or imprison criminals. Justice will be swift. The first strike is a warning. Second strike will be physical punishment based on the severity of the offense. I hate to do it, but it's fast, it serves as a deterrent, and once it's done, all is forgiven. Third strike and you're cast out. If you can't follow the rules, if you can't be a productive member of our community, you can try your luck out on the road. That's the deal.

Finally, rule number seven. All Companions are equal. I'm not your Sheriff anymore. I'm just your Companion. We are all Companions now.

We've got a new world to build, so get some breakfast and let's get to work. That's it.

***

Clearing the yard was slow. Nap insisted on leading the effort, despite the bandages covering his eye. The only creepers left were so damaged or decomposed that they could barely move, but that didn't stop them from trying to take a bite if anyone got too close. The Kill Squad recruited willing townspeople for a search line, shoulder-to-shoulder, covering every inch of the yard. Every tent had to be checked, every corpse removed, every car opened and searched. Even the snow presented a danger. Four inches of white fluff was enough to completely cover a body. Every odd lump had to be approached with caution, just in case.

Julia and I spent the day cleaning the lab.

The creepers had left all the rooms in the science wing alone, except the lab. Maybe Mr. Bowness called to them, or maybe there was enough of a human smell to make it stand out, but they'd gotten in, and Mr. Bowness was gone.

These creepers dripped less. In Lochshire, the herd left a slimy snail trail of fluids everywhere they went, but this herd hardly left a drop, just the occasional bloody handprint or smear. Maybe it was the cold affecting them, or maybe these creepers had already dripped all they were going to drip, oozed all they were going to ooze.

They destroyed all the tissue samples, and the freezer was left open. It had thawed and water had pooled on the floor around it. The incubator was smashed on the ground, broken glass everywhere. All the glass trays were opened and the samples were gone. *Had they eaten them?*

We righted the incubator and reassembled the shelves, but most of the glassware was shattered. The hinges on the door were damaged, so it didn't seal properly, which we could work around, but the digital thermostat was smashed. It was the sensor that switched the heating unit on and off to maintain the correct temperature. The incubator would just cook our samples until we got a replacement part, which would slow any progress.

Without the Capitol, we were on our own. That made the work seem more urgent, but we couldn't do anything without tissue samples. There was plenty of dead tissue around, but without an incubator, there was no way to study living tissue, and I didn't know where she was going to get more.

By the end of the day, the seven rules were painted above the memorial near the main entrance.

> 1) We don't kill the living.
> 2) We don't forget the dead.
> 3) Everyone eats.
> 4) Everyone who works gets a vote.
> 5) Everyone is always on watch.
> 6) Three strikes and you're out.
> 7) All Companions are equal.

There was a new list of names on the memorial. After Companions, Unfortunates, and Absent was the heading "Martyrs." Below Steven Winters, Freddy Wozzeck and Matt Cordell, added unceremoniously, almost an afterthought, was the true hero we owed our independence to: John Pike.

Chapter Thirty-Two: Proposals

Things changed after the Major was gone. Important decisions were made at the weekly General Assemblies. Miss Styx called it a "consensus process." Everyone could express their opinion, but only people who worked were free to make proposals, and vote on them. Each proposal was discussed. If there were objections, we would try to reach a compromise, but ultimately everything was put to a majority vote. Work details were still posted at the Armory every morning, but instead of an assigned schedule, people volunteered on a signup sheet.

The community was split on almost every proposal and people lined up to argue for and against everything. There was no official rule, but Nap usually held his opinion until the end. If they couldn't reach a compromise, he could usually persuade enough people to break a tie with a rousing speech.

Nap's eye healed enough to remove the bandages. His face was bruised black and purple, and the bloodshot eye had faded to a dull yellow. The pupil stayed constricted and never fully dilated again. He lost most of his vision in that eye, and it wandered, never quite pointing the same way as the other. It looked like a creeper's eye.

Being Julia's lab assistant counted as work, and sometimes I volunteered to keep watch. There were always four Watchers on duty; two with experience and two trainees. I was always considered a trainee, because of my age, but I fired a gun better than most of them. When my bandages came off, everything sounded like the volume was turned down on one side, which messed with my sense of the direction a sound was coming from, but at least I could still hear.

By the next General Assembly, there were dozens of proposals. They started having General Assemblies every day to keep up.

They changed the bell system to one dawn bell, one lunch bell, and one dusk bell. It passed almost unanimously because tying the schedule to the sun saved power. Everyone agreed that all the surveillance cameras should be pointed outside, although the original proposal was to shut them off. That was the compromise.

A proposal to paint "SOS" on the roof passed unanimously, although a smoke signal was voted down. A proposal to create water reserves from snow passed after some people expressed fears that the well water might be contaminated.

The yard was clear, but no one wanted to live in the tents. It was cold and people were still afraid, but there was plenty of work in the yard. Snow had to be shoveled. Supplies had to be inventoried. Volunteers walked the perimeter to clear any creepers along the fence.

A proposal to remove the fences in the hallway and use them to reinforce the outside barricades was very contentious. It passed with a narrow majority, but only after they agreed that Watchers would sound the lockdown alarm at the first sign of a breach. That would signal everyone in the yard to rush inside, take defensive positions, and await instructions over the PA system.

We practiced that drill every day at lunch. When the bell went off, everyone stopped and sprinted to their predetermined positions. Most people were assigned to secure areas, like the library. The Kill Squad was assigned to guard stations on the roof, or gun ports in the walls. Each position was equipped with a radio to report their readiness to Nap in the security office. No one ate until every position had checked in, and he read our response time over the PA system.

By the second week, General Assemblies passed more proposals than we had volunteers, and people who didn't support a proposal refused to do the work, even if it passed. The signup sheets got longer, but less got done. A proposal to build a windmill was tabled after a week without a single sign-up. Another proposal to reposition abandoned cars into a barrier passed unanimously, but no one wanted to do the work.

At least half the proposals that passed never got done. People quickly figured out that if they wanted a project to get done, they usually had to do the work themselves. That meant the people who wanted to work had to get permission from the people who refused to work. Moses wanted to get back to grave digging, and there was plenty to do, but the dissenters wouldn't allow it unless he agreed to chop firewood. That was the compromise made by people who wouldn't do either job.

Lots of people stopped working all together. It was in the rules, "Everyone eats." So, people ate whether they worked or not, and many of them gave up their vote rather than work a hard job.

Tension was high. One morning, Nap announced that rule number four was changed from "Everyone who works gets a vote" to simply "Everyone works. Everyone votes." But that change caused more problems. People signed up for easy jobs first, leaving tougher jobs for last. When the Major was in charge, he gave Staci jobs appropriate to her ability, but under the new approach, the only jobs left were usually impossible for her.

Livia was expecting her baby before Christmas and was in no condition to work, but she was made to anyway. One day, while cleaning the cafeteria, she collapsed from exhaustion. Mrs. Mills assured everyone that she was fine, and the baby was healthy, she was just malnourished.

At the next General Assembly, Mrs. Mills proposed that Livia be given extra rations and bedrest until the baby came. It was overwhelmingly voted down. Detractors insisted it was Livia's responsibility to propose jobs she could do, not their responsibility to give her special treatment. The debate erupted into a full-blown protest. A dozen Companions walked out of the meeting, led by Livia's husband, Andre. They occupied Nap's office, refusing to leave until Rule Four was restored to the original.

All the protestors were given their first strike and threatened with laundry duty if they didn't disperse. Nap said they were, "inciting anarchy."

After the crowd settled, Julia proposed a compromise that Mrs. Mills would have the authority to excuse people from work for medical reasons, and everyone agreed. The injured, elderly, and those with special needs were excused from work. Livia was given rest, but no extra food. So Andre gave her half his rations.

Soon, there was an epidemic of minor medical issues in Thornhaven. Chronic fatigue, arthritis, insomnia, restless leg syndrome, anxiety, and more. The nurse's office was overwhelmed with people seeking a medical exemption from work.

It wasn't all bad news. People were taking security into their own hands, and that made them less fearful. Training more townspeople to keep watch and use firearms meant more Watchers and Runners for the Sheriff's Kill Squad.

Members of the Kill Squad got special treatment. They were served first at meals, given more leisure time, better living accommodations, and they were exempted from other work, but they couldn't opt out. Once drafted onto the Kill Squad, they were expected to follow orders, until death.

More Runners meant more supply runs, but not necessarily more supplies. Everything nearby had already been searched and Runners had to venture further out to find anything.

Occasionally, the Runners found signs of other survivors, like empty cans, and cold fire pits, but no one alive.

Simon, the boxer, quickly became the hardest worker in Thornhaven, easily doing the physical labor of two men. He hauled lumber, raised wall segments, and when necessary, crushed skulls. He was a gentle giant, responding to every criticism and complaint with a promise to try harder.

Classes started again, but there was no official curriculum. The faculty wanted students to learn basic math and literacy, but everyone else was eager for young people to work. Most classes were for adults. Anyone with any expertise taught it to others, but people wanted to learn subjects no one knew about. What's the best way to make bricks from clay? How does blacksmithing work? Could we make our own bows and arrows? We were rebuilding from the ground up, which meant we had to go back to basics. The library became the workshop for that exploration.

Everyone felt a new satisfaction knowing they controlled their own destiny.

Stinky loved the new setup. With the yard unoccupied, it was his personal playground. People saw him but they couldn't catch him, so he became familiar. Kids brought him food to lure him over. He understood the game, darting forward and back, but never letting them catch him. The community was less paranoid, and they stopped worrying he might carry infection, except Julia, who thought he should be dissected.

He'd found some way to get in and out of the school. Moses fed him scraps from the cafeteria, and he chased rats out of the pantry. On cold nights, he snuggled with me under my blanket, but he disappeared before the first bell to avoid other kids.

When I had watch duty on the roof, I was usually partnered with Nap or Andre, and Stinky would join us. Sometimes he was feeling playful, but he mostly just curled up in my lap by the fire. He was our early warning system. Even when he was asleep, the slightest rustle in the yard woke him instantly, and he'd run to the edge of the roof. It was usually a small animal and he'd leap off the roof and go after it, but if it was a creeper, he'd howl at us, and someone would go take care of it.

Stinky hunted birds and squirrels. Once he caught a garden snake, but mostly he caught rats. Often, he brought them to me as gifts.

PorcScouts Rule #5, *Use Everything. Waste Nothing.*

I decided to preserve the meat and add it to my bug-out bag. Most people would be disgusted by the thought of eating rat. They think they're filthy and carry disease, but that's just the reality of city life. Rural rats are just as healthy as any wild game. Some cultures regularly eat rat, and I'd eaten pigeon. Sooner or later, it always comes down to food. Saving meat—any meat—for an emergency was a no-brainer.

My PorcScouts Survival Guide had a chapter on rabbit meat, but the instructions were easily adaptable for rats.

The first section was on humane slaughter. For raising or trapping rabbits, or in case of an incomplete kill while hunting, a quick death is desired to minimize the suffering. It recommended a swift slice across the animal's throat, to sever the jugular vein and carotid arteries, then allowing the blood to drain.

In this case, the critters that Stinky brought were already dead. Regardless of how humanely they died, it was the natural order. Everything is food for something else.

The Survival Guild described skinning small game in three steps. I used the knife on my multi-tool. It was small and sharp, like a scalpel, so it was perfect.

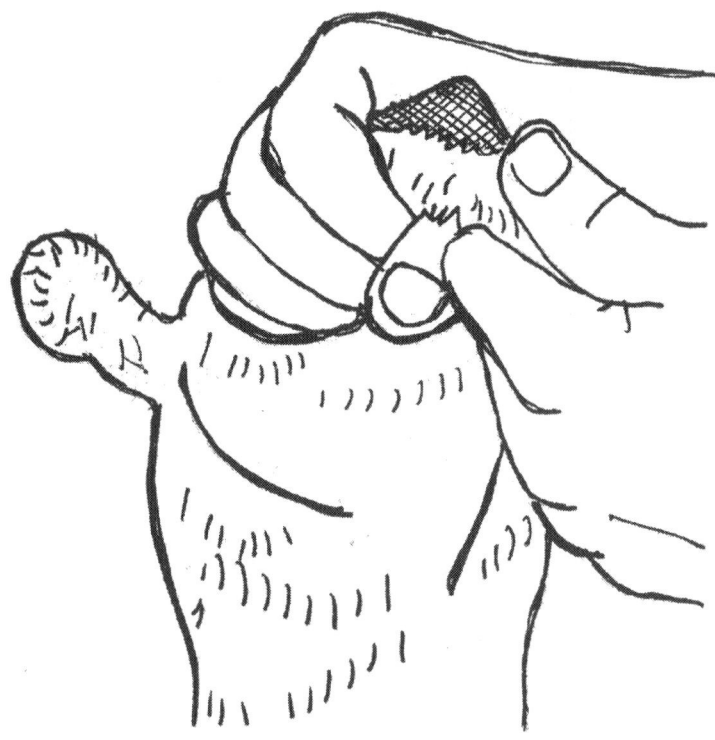

1) Bend each front foot forward, cutting across the back of the knuckle to release the joint. Cut through the joint to remove the front feet.

The front legs were small, and had almost no meat, so it was easier to just slice them off. When Stinky brought me a critter, the first thing I did was give him the front legs. Sometimes I threw them over his head and he'd snatch them out of the air, or I'd make him tug them out of my hands with his teeth. Then he'd sit by the fire and chew them down to the bone.

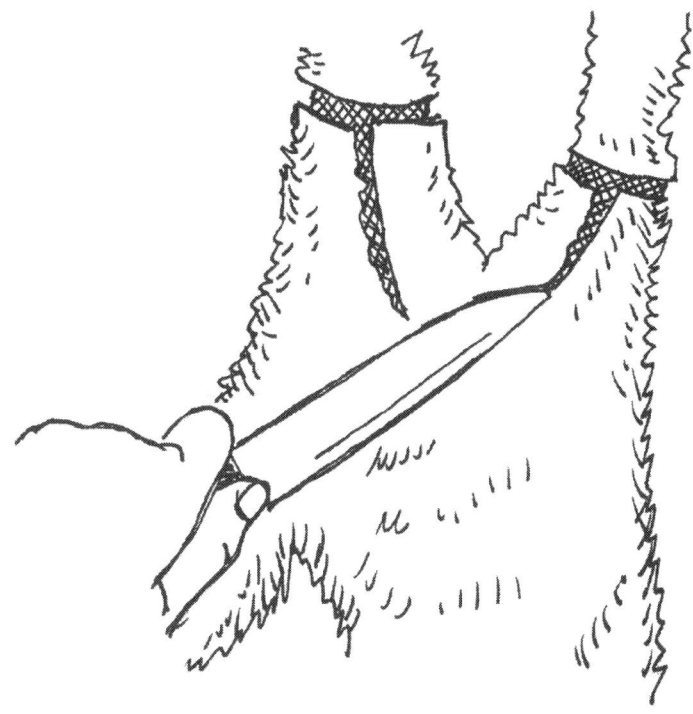

2) Cut a ring around each back ankle to separate the hide of the legs from the hide of the feet. Slice down the length of each leg from the ring cuts, connecting at the base of the tail.

This cut was especially difficult because the rats were so small. Half the time, I would accidentally cut off a back foot, or puncture the bladder or intestine and soil the meat. It was easier to make a single incision along the spine from shoulders to hips, to avoid the stomach entirely.

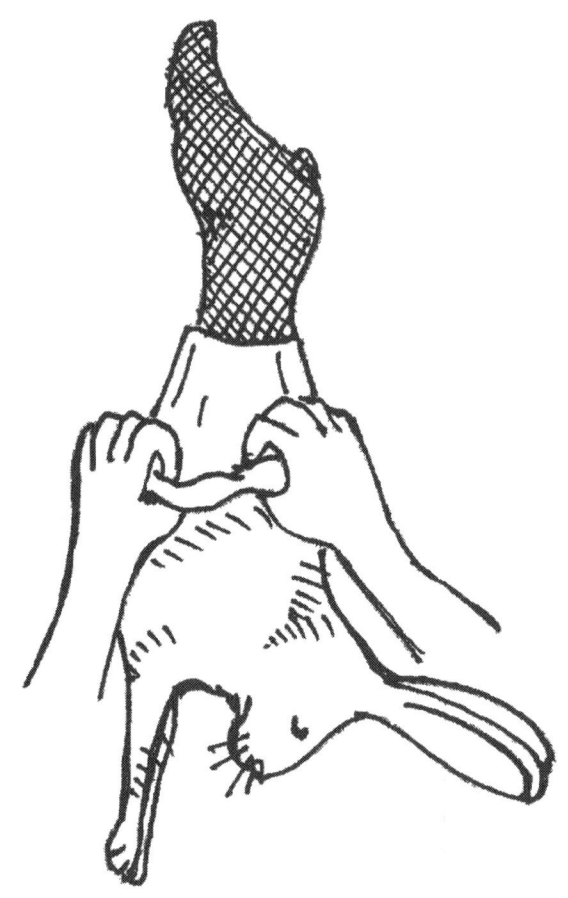

*3) Starting from the ring cuts, peel the hide
down the legs. At the tailbone, grab each side of the
hide and pull down the body. Cut away connective
tissue where necessary.*

I was surprised how fast the hide slipped off. I had to be careful
not to tear it. It was easier to push gently with my fingertips, instead
of pulling the hide like the book described, almost like rolling off a
sock. I sliced the tail off, and cut around the ears and nose. I got so
good I could slide off the whole pelt as one inside-out sleeve.

I took the innards out last to avoid contaminating the meat. I'd
split the chest and scoop the guts out with my finger. Most of the

organs came out with a little tug, but I had to cut a few bits that hung on with connective tissue. The Survival Guide recommended cutting the liver open to look for signs of parasites or disease, and then the meat was ready to cook. I stored the meat in cold water while I cleaned up.

By that time, Stinky would be done gnawing on the front legs and came back for the head, which I removed by severing the neck. Stinky wouldn't go for the head unless I cracked it open, so he could eat the brain. I think that was half the reason he brought me rats.

I threw whatever unwanted parts Stinky wouldn't eat in the fire.

With any larger critters, I'd remove each limb at the hips and shoulders, and cut off any significant portions of meat, like the breast of a chicken, or the back strap of a rabbit, but the rats were too small for that. I rinsed off any hair or blood and skewered the whole carcass on a stick from neck to tail.

The first ones I cooked by holding them over the fire. They were gamey, but edible. The other Watchers wouldn't try it.

I flipped to the chapter on preserving meat:

> *Why does meat spoil? Exactly what we are fighting? Bacteria is the number one cause of spoilage. When preserving meat, that is the enemy. Bacteria needs warmth and moisture to thrive. Removing moisture from the meat removes the bacteria's home. Storing meat below 65° F will slow bacteria growth, and freezing meat will stop it. Unfortunately, bacteria growth starts again as soon as the meat thaws. Similarly, temperatures over 100° F will slow bacteria growth, and temperatures over 200° F will destroy it.*

That was the same temperature window we needed for an incubator in the lab, which made perfect sense. The incubator was intended to be an ideal environment for microorganisms.

The section on drying meat described cutting it into strips and hanging it in the sun, but it'd have to be protected from birds and insects. Another section was on marinating it in brine, or salting the meat, which added flavor, but I didn't have those supplies. I could freeze the meat in the lab, but cross contamination was too great a risk. Smoking the meat was the best solution.

> *Prior to refrigeration, people would smoke or salt their meat. Smoke is a natural preservative. Most family farms had a "smokehouse," and smokers are still readily available for people with a taste for smoked meat, but most smoked meat still requires refrigeration.*
>
> *To preserve meat without refrigeration, it must be dried and smoked until it's similar to jerky. In addition, many household spices inhibit bacteria growth. Common spices include salt, garlic, ginger, pepper, oregano, cinnamon, cayenne, horseradish, and many others. When done properly, meat can be preserved indefinitely, but its quality will deteriorate over time. It is best to eat it within a year.*

The instructions were simple. A moist hardwood would give a good smoke. It listed hickory, cherry, and apple. Softwoods have too much pitch. Moses had been collecting sugar maple for the furnace. It's what Watchers used in the fire pits. Sugar maple is a hardwood.

To prep the meat, it said to remove all visible fat, since it doesn't preserve well, and can spoil the meat. The rats had hardly any fat on them, anyway. Simon brought me a large bottle of soy sauce he found on a run, which made an excellent salty marinade.

Most of the chapter was about different smoking methods. Cold smoking never reaches a temperature high enough to kill bacteria. Wet smoking keeps the meat too moist. Dry smoking has to be kept under 160° F so the meat dries rather than cooks. Most of that wasn't useful in my situation, but I knew Dad. He prepared for the worst case scenario. At the end of the chapter was a section on field smoking.

> *For smoking in the field, the best method is to build a tripod, with a shelf constructed halfway up. The shelf should be a grid pattern to allow airflow around the meat. Never use galvanized steel. It will poison the meat. Construct a simple canopy over the tripod to hold the smoke. Place the structure over a small, smoky fire. Watch the fire to make sure it doesn't get too hot. The goal is to produce smoke, not heat. Building an improvised drying structure is only limited by the materials available in your environment and your imagination.*

I built mine out of yard sticks from a classroom, and two rain ponchos as a canopy. I started a small, controlled fire using damp wood to produce a good, heavy smoke. I borrowed a thermometer from the science lab to monitor the temperature.

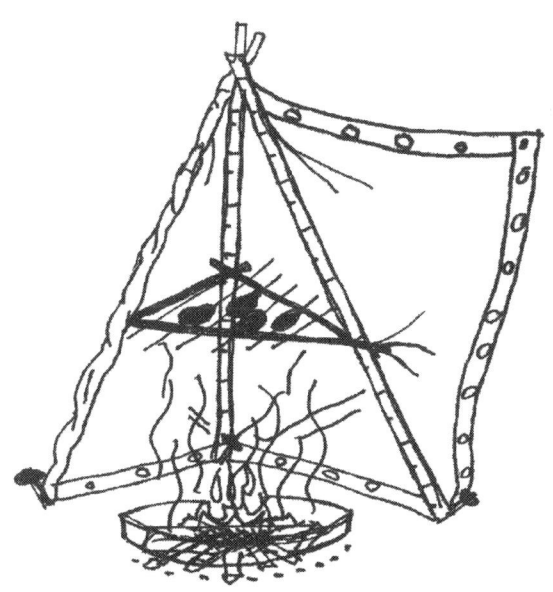

Following the instructions, I kept the smoke thick and the temperature between 120° and 160° F until the meat was dark and brittle. Then I added dry wood and raised the temperature to over 200° F for half an hour to fully destroy any bacteria. It took about six hours, and could be finished in one watch shift.

The finished rats were nice and crispy, and when they cooled, the meat pulled off the bones easily. They had a smoky flavor with a touch of salt from the soy sauce and a hint of sweetness from the sugar maple.

When the other Watchers got a whiff of cooking meat, they were eager to try it. Before long, it was an open secret that anyone on duty with me would get a taste. It was a time-consuming process, but on long nights, it was a productive way to pass the time.

No one ever complained to me about it. Nap seemed amused by it and said it was a "harmless hobby." After a week of perfecting my process and building my supply, I received a pink Disciplinary Referral in my locker. It was the first sign that anyone objected.

It was the same form teachers sent to parents of problem students before the collapse. At the top of it was "Notice To Parents: The purpose of this notice is to inform you of a disciplinary incident involving your student." Under "Student's Name" was handwritten "Max Hartwell," under "Class" was "Night Watch," and under "Teacher" was "Anonymous Informant."

The first section was "Reason(s) for This Notice" and someone wrote, "Food preparation without permission or equitable redistribution."

The second section was "Present Action(s) Taken." "Student Reprimanded" was checked, and "This is your first strike. See me for clarification," was written.

The last section was "Future Action Recommendation(s)" and "Grave Digging" was written in.

It was signed by Miss Styx. I went to her office and she explained that she received an anonymous complaint, prompting the warning, but wouldn't tell me who ratted me out. She said I could only continue if all the meat was delivered to the cafeteria to share with everyone. She said, "Every Companion has an obligation to contribute all they can to the common stock, and to take out only as much as they need."

From then on, I brought the rat jerky to the cafeteria where they boiled it into a mystery meat stew. That way, it was easy to redistribute, and every bit of nutrients were used. Canned vegetables were added to stretch the meal, and after the meat was gone, you could still taste it in the broth. I still stashed a few morsels of meat from every cook in my bug-out bag, just in case.

Chapter Thirty-Four: Discontent

Sometimes, I stopped to look at the memorial in the hall. So many people were still missing. We didn't know if they were alive or dead. I still wondered if the other PorcScouts ever made it to the cabin. At night, I'd scroll through the channels on Dad's radio, but I never picked up any signal. If it were warmer, I could make it to the cabin and still get back before dark if it wasn't safe, but the snow made it a hard road. I knew if they were alive, they were warm and fed. We trained for this, and the cabin felt like home.

I had an important role in Thornhaven, a lab to work in, and a research partner, but even with the Major gone, I couldn't shake the feeling that something was wrong. I didn't belong. The PorcScouts were the closest thing I had to family, and I was determined to go find them when the snow melted.

The General Assemblies had become incredibly time-consuming. Everyone was allowed to speak, and people held up the process by rambling off topic. The assemblies were so boring and unproductive that many stopped coming, while others took advantage of the low attendance to cram through proposals the majority wouldn't support. They forced people into the refugee tents, scheduled black outs, and shut the hot water off to save power. Nap started including all proposals in the morning announcements, so people had no excuse for not knowing, and he announced that even though attending was voluntary, those who ditched would get half rations that day.

They formed workgroups that handled certain types of proposals, to alleviate the burden on the General Assembly. The Safe Space workgroup was in charge of reinforcing the fences; the Abundance workgroup handled food distribution; and the Maintenance workgroup did repairs, laundry, waste, yardwork, and other daily chores.

That didn't solve the problem. It made General Assemblies shorter, but less effective, because proposals had to be approved by a committee before going to the General Assembly. There was also infighting. The Safe Space committee and the Maintenance committee were in constant disputes over tools and materials. The Kill Squad insisted they should be exempt from the reduced rations set by the Abundance committee, since their job was so dangerous.

To resolve disputes between workgroups, they elected a Leadership Committee consisting of Nap, Miss Styx, and Mr. Ash. The Leadership Committee claimed the authority to strike down any proposal that conflicted with their long-term plans. They also granted each workgroup the same power to bypass the signup sheet and draft workers for important jobs.

No matter what they did, there never seemed to be enough food. Rations were modest in the morning and miniscule in the evening. Sometimes, dinner was no more than potato chips and peanut butter. It made workers weak and tempers short. I missed the days of canned peaches and corn chowder at Lochshire. If something didn't change, we wouldn't survive the winter.

I proposed hunting in the woods behind the school. There would be rabbits, pheasants, and probably deer. I figured everyone would appreciate some fresh meat after weeks of pink slime. We could even tan the skins and make winter clothes. It was voted down.

Instead, the Leadership Committee announced that every General Assembly would begin with the Anthem of Thornhaven. They had everyone stand, face the Thornhaven flag, and put their hand over their heart. Everyone recited the anthem in dull tones.

I didn't stand.

Staci and Holland nudged me, but I refused. When Miss Styx noticed, she stopped the whole group. "Max, you need to stand with the rest of the group."

I crossed my arms. "I choose to sit."

"If you're not going to recite the Anthem with everyone else, I'm going to have to ask you to leave." I started to leave. "And you'll get half rations for skipping the General Assembly."

I stopped. "Why should I go hungry just for not singing your stupid song? I'm not hurting anybody. I got a right sit quietly if I want to. Nobody died and made you queen!"

The room was stunned.

She bristled. "The Leadership Committee unanimously agreed that reciting the Anthem would be good for community unity."

"You can't eat community!" I countered. "We don't need songs, and we don't need more committees. We need food. If we can't scavenge enough food, we should be hunting."

"You are out of order!" she yelled. "If you want to propose something food related, you have to respect the process! Not until it passes the Abundance committee, and not until we've all recited the Anthem."

"Fine, then answer this. How is a Leadership Committee not a violation of rule seven? How can all Companions be equal if some are more equal than others? I don't get to write songs and force you to sing them!"

Scott was the first person to sit down, followed by Holland and others.

"The Companions elected the Leadership Committee!" yelled Miss Styx. "You should have raised your objections before the proposal passed. If you didn't vote, you have no right to complain."

"I voted no!"

"Well, then you have to respect the will of the majority. If you don't like it, you can leave."

"Fine! I'll get my things and go."

"What?" Her eyes widened. "You can't leave, it's not safe!"

"So I'm a prisoner here?"

"Enough!" Nap interrupted. "Max doesn't have to stand if he doesn't want to. Max, you will respect those who choose to stand, or you'll be asked to leave the General Assembly, and you will receive half rations for the day. I don't want to hear any more about leaving. Equality doesn't mean no leaders. A community without leadership is a community without a central plan. It's doomed to fail. All seven rules are derived from one simple

148

principle. The common needs of the Thornhaven community are more important than the needs of any individual Companion. Good leaders make decisions for the general welfare, not for some selfish benefit. If people don't think we're being effective, they should elect new leaders, but you can't vote for no leaders. That would be anarchy. Let's table these distractions. We've got important business to get to."

Chapter Thirty-Five: Grave Digging

I earned a second strike for the outburst. Nap tried to talk Miss Styx down, but she insisted that I be punished for disrupting the General Assembly. Mr. Ash sided with her, so Nap was outvoted, but he talked them into a lenient punishment. I was sentenced to a day of grave digging with Moses. Nap asked me to go along with it to keep the peace, and assured me that he considered me an asset to the community.

The furnace wasn't hot enough to destroy the bones, so Moses made tombstones using the nameplates from the memorial and buried the remains in the yard.

"Moses, can I ask you something?"

"Go ahead. Dese folks eh in no hurry." He rested on his shovel.

"You made headstones for Matt Cordell, Major Winters, and Private Woz, but I know there are no bodies in those graves."

"Yuh know bout dat, huh?" He spit. "Ah know dey not dead for sure, but dey dead to us. A cemetery ain't bout de bodies. Time and nature take care of dem, even when dey walkin arong. It's bout makin people feel like deat is bein taken care of. Dat's why dey doh care if we don work so hard, as long as we out here. Dey want to feel like someone is tinkin bout der loved ones, even when dey forget. Like someone will tink bout dem. It doh matter if di body in de ground. It doh even really matter if dey alive or dead. At de end of de day, we all walkin dead ahready. Always was. Notin changed. We juss givin people closure."

We spent the morning digging and mounting nameplates to chunks of granite. There was a clear sky, and the air was crisp, but not too cold. The work kept us warm. It was soothing, almost relaxing, and it helped me clear my head.

I dug a grave for Dad, even though he wasn't part of Thornhaven. Moses said, "Yuh fadda is a part of you, an you is a part of we. A grave is wort diggin even if it only comfortin de one diggin it. Eh no good to clear de jumbies from de yard if we doh clear de ghosts from we heads. People put tings on graves like 'Rest in peace' or 'Love lives on,' like dey speaking to de dead. Ah like to tink is de dead speakin to we, tellin us to find peace witout regret, an love witout fear."

"What should I bury?"

"Anyting yuh like. You doh have to bury notting. Sometimes is enough juss to dig."

I considered burying our family photo, but it was the only one I had, or maybe Dad's radio, but it was too useful. There was nothing of his that I could afford to part with, not the Survival Guide, not any of my gear. I decided someday I'd go back to Lochshire and put his body to rest.

The fence rattled behind me. There was a creeper at the fence, a man in a red apron and cornflower blue tie. The flesh was blown off one side of its jaw, like someone shot it in the mouth but missed the brain. A name tag on its apron read, "Shop Smart. Shop S-Mart," with "Ned" underneath.

Moses walked up to it and Ned shook the fence. He waved to the Watchers on the roof, who were already aiming at Ned. "Ah got dis!"

Moses scratched his beard, sizing Ned up. He snapped his fingers in Ned's face to get its attention, and with the other hand, he picked Ned's pocket.

"Max, come look at dis." He opened Ned's wallet and pulled out a Georgia driver's license. "Edwyn Paulan," he read. "Dat weird. Ned muss be he nickname. He died wit twenty eight dollars, an a picture of a pretty girl." He flipped the photo over. "Valerie," he read. "Suppose Valerie alive. Ned look like he was at work when it happen. S-Mart juss a few miles away. Bet she doh know what happen to him." Moses flipped his shovel around. The end of the handle was carved into a spike. He stabbed Ned in the eye through the fence. "Leh we take a walk."

We walked the perimeter, all the way around to get Ned's body. "If Ah ever find Valerie, I go tell she wha happen to Ned," he said. "An if Ah don't, Ah tink someday, somebody go find a well-marked grave dat will put dere min at peace."

We tagged the body and put it in a pile of corpses set to be brought to the boiler room.

There was no headstone for Ellie.

The next morning, the Maintenance staff was searching through everyone's stuff. "Mr. Nap has ordered a surprise inspection of the whole camp," Mr. Ash explained. Something was stolen and they were determined to find it. They found lots of contraband, mostly snacks, and those people were given strikes, but the search continued.

They took us to the locker room in groups to search our stuff. Mr. Ash supervised, checking off locker numbers on his clipboard. He wouldn't tell us what was stolen.

"Max Hartwell, you're next. Open it up," ordered Mr. Ash. I unlocked it, confident they wouldn't find anything. Everything was hidden in the secret compartment.

They tossed all my things out on the ground and moved on.

I was picking everything up and putting it away as the next group came in. They were in the next row of lockers, but my ears perked up when I heard the next name on Mr. Ash's list.

"Niles Perry?" read Mr. Ash, but he got no response. "Where's Niles?"

Holland spoke up. "I'm his brother. I use his locker now. He's dead."

"Good to know." Mr. Ash scratched out Niles' name and wrote in Holland's name. "Okay. Open it up."

I closed my locker and came around the corner to watch.

Holland unlocked it and let them search. They removed all his personal possessions and dropped them on the floor. They pulled out his clothes, shoes, comic books, a towel, a digital camera, the AV club keys, and a black digital camera case.

"Let me see that." Mr. Ash grabbed the case and opened it.

"Stop!" cried Holland. "That's mine. You've got no right!" He lunged forward, but the staff held him back.

Mr. Ash pulled out matches, cracked reading glasses, and the bundle of wax paper. "What's this?"

"Don't! It's all I have left!" Holland begged.

Mr. Ash slowly unwrapped the paper, and something slipped out and fell onto the floor. Everyone gasped. Mr. Ash covered his mouth as he examined it.

It was a severed human finger.

Holland wept. "You can't take it! You just can't!"

Mr. Ash touched Holland's shoulder. "Son, I can't let you keep this." He wrapped the finger and put it in his pocket. "It's a biohazard. It has to be burned with the other bodies."

"It's all I have. It's everything!" Holland yelled.

"Son, I'm not going to give you a strike for this, but I'm going to recommend mandatory counseling with Miss Styx. You need to talk to someone about losing your brother."

A staff member escorted Holland out while another crammed his stuff back into his locker.

Mr. Ash checked his clipboard. "Next up… the broken locker." He pulled out the master key, and my heart pounded as he tried the lock, but it was good and jammed.

"Anyone got a crowbar?" he asked.

I swallowed. "There's no point. Nobody's used it since before the collapse."

"Better safe than sorry," he countered. "And once it's open, maybe someone can fix it." Someone from the Maintenance staff brought him a crowbar and he wedged it in the frame.

I was sweating, that third strike hanging over my head.

Mr. Ash pulled hard but it didn't budge. "Man! This thing's really stuck." He got on the other side, and put all his weight pushing on it. The metal creaked as the door strained. I covered my ears, expecting a clang when it popped.

"Mr. Ash! Over here." A man came in with a duffel bag. "Look at this."

Mr. Ash relaxed and pulled out the crowbar. I let out a breath. They opened the duffel and it was filled with canned food.

"That's the stuff," said Mr. Ash. "Where'd you find it?"

Andre had been stealing food for Livia. He insisted malnourishment was a risk for the baby. Nurse Mills warned them about the dangers of a low birth weight, but the Abundance committee wouldn't even let his proposals for extra rations reach the General Assembly because it had already been shot down. Nurse Mills, Andre, and others had shared their rations with her, but as people got hungry and supplies ran short, so did their generosity. Livia was dangerously underweight. Andre said he had no choice but to steal.

He got a second strike. That meant physical punishment.

It wasn't right away. There were murmurs and whispers. The community didn't know what to expect, and lots of people were convinced they wouldn't go through with it, but at the next General Assembly, Nap proposed that Andre get ten lashes in front of everyone.

"We must protect the rule of law," he said. "Otherwise, we invite anarchy. Theft is unacceptable. An example must be made."

It was put to a general vote, but Miss Styx and Mr. Ash raised their arms in favor of it immediately, without any discussion, as if they planned it. Their votes weren't nearly enough to clinch a decision, but no one wanted to oppose a unanimous Leadership. There was no debate, and no dissenting votes except for mine, but more than half the people didn't vote.

Andre was ordered to remove his shirt and place his palms against the wall. He glanced around, as if asking if there were really no objections. He walked defiantly, and took his shirt off. His ribs were plain to see from across the room, and his pants were cinched around his protruding hip bones.

Nap had made a whip out of woven electrical cords and he handled it like a rancher. He said to Andre, "Son, this is gonna hurt, but it hurts me more to have to do it. I hope you know why I have to."

The first crack knocked the wind out of Andre. He grunted, and pressed his fists against the wall. When the pain passed, he opened his palms again and gasped.

The second crack of the whip snapped hard; Andre groaned. His whole body clenched and trembled, and then he relaxed again, breathing in heaves.

The crowd moaned in horror. No one had ever seen anything like it.

On the third crack, Andre let out a short yawp as his body gave in and he fell to his knees.

"Get him up," Mr. Nap ordered Simon and Moses.

Moses shook his head and folded his arms across his chest. "No, suh."

Nap pointed the whip at Moses. "That's your warning." He pointed at Scott. "You, get him up."

Simon and Scott moved toward Andre, but he held out his hand to stop them, and stood up on his own.

Andre tensed before the fourth lash landed, and he took it. On the fifth, he fell to his hands and knees sobbing, "Mercy!"

There was a pause. I thought Nap would stop. Five was half. He'd made his point, but he motioned to Simon and Scott. "Go on. Get him up." They grabbed Andre's arms and pulled him to his feet. When they let go, he slumped back down. "Hold him up if you have to," he ordered.

They picked him up and pushed him against the wall, holding his arms out. Cracks six and seven came quickly, and Andre sobbed and convulsed. He tried to pull away but they held him.

After the eighth crack, there was a splash of red as the whip broke skin. Andre screamed and shook. Scott's eyes begged Nap to stop.

Nap was ready to swipe again when Andre grunted, "Wait! I think," he gulped. "I think I'm…" He leaned forward and vomited on the wall. Simon and Scott backed away, and Andre dropped into the puddle of bile.

Nap covered his mouth, and looked like he might be sick, too. "That's enough," he whispered. "Take him to the nurse's office and get him cleaned up. Tell him all is forgiven. I'm going," he gulped. "I'll be in my office."

Moses and Mrs. Mills carried Andre out, and Nap left without staying for the rest of the General Assembly.

Chapter Thirty-Seven: Simon the Boxer

The next morning, Andre was supposed to relieve me from watch duty, but he never showed up. Then Livia wasn't at breakfast. I went to look for them, but their room was empty, and the Burke rifle was missing from the Armory. They were gone.

The mood in Thornhaven was solemn after that. Everyone was afraid to talk about the lashing, and when Nap was around, most people just kept their heads down and worked.

Nap assembled the Kill Squad for a big run, and after they left, everyone breathed easy.

People whispered about where they thought Andre and Livia went. Most people hoped they went south, to Spooner Memorial Hospital in Plymouth. If there were survivors there, maybe they'd find a doctor. Some people hoped they went farther north, to White Mountain Ski Resort in Lincoln, where they'd at least be warm through the winter. Both of those places were more than ten miles away. I was worried that no matter where they went, they were in no condition to travel on foot in the snow.

I spent the morning shift on watch, covering for Andre, and then slept through lunch. After that, Julia and I spent the afternoon sorting our new samples by age and decomposition. We still hadn't found the parts we needed to repair the incubator, so we had to freeze everything.

Near dusk, Nap kicked the door and charged into the room. He was holding Simon, who was limping and wincing in pain. They were covered in blood.

"Make room!" Nap yelled.

"What's going on?" asked Julia.

He laid Simon on a lab station. "He's been bit! You've got to amputate!"

"What? I don't have the equipment. Where's Mrs. Mills?"

"Her hands are full treating gunshots. You've gotta do it here, and you've got to do it now!" He drew a knife and cut away Simon's pant leg. A chunk was torn away above Simon's knee.

"Gunshots!?" She removed her belt. "Max, grab the hacksaw out of my tool box. Go. Now!"

I ran.

"What happened?" She cinched the belt around Simon's leg.

"We were attacked. Gunfire drew the dead-heads." He held Simon's leg down and said to him, "This is gonna hurt, Son, but we're not gonna lose you."

Simon nodded. I rushed back and handed Julia the hacksaw.

"I didn't hear any gunshots," said Julia, as she set the saw above the wound.

"We were at the S-Mart in Campton."

"Campton!" She stopped. "That's four miles away. How long has it been?"

"An hour, hour and a half tops."

She set down the saw. "Mr. Nap, it's too late."

"Too late? We have to try! We have to do something!" he yelled.

Simon was calm.

"I'm sorry. There's nothing we can do. I won't torture him for no reason." She released the belt.

"It's okay, Sheriff," Simon said between breaths. "I've given a good life."

"Dammit!" Nap pounded on the desk and lifted his knife toward Simon's head.

"Stop!" I screamed. "Simon, you still have time. Isn't there anything you want to do? Anyone to say goodbye to?"

Simon paused. "No, I don't have anyone."

"You're a good man, Simon. One of our best," said Nap. "We all owe you a great debt for your service."

"I'm ready." Simon closed his eyes and clenched his jaw.

Nap brought the knife to Simon's head. "Wait." Julia stopped him. "Let me observe him. Let me record the change."

Nap looked skeptical.

She turned to Simon. "I'll make sure you're comfortable and taken care of after. Please, let me do this. You have no idea what an opportunity this is."

Simon nodded. "Anything to help."

We cleaned and bandaged his wound so he stayed healthy as long as possible, but he insisted that we shouldn't waste medical supplies on him.

Nap moved a security camera into the lab to monitor from his office in case something went wrong.

Julia and I scheduled tests to track the transformation. We took hourly blood samples and conducted cognitive tests every two hours, with basic questions like whether he knew his name and if he could read a clock. It was followed by complex tasks like solving a maze and word associations. Every other hour, we conducted physical tests of his reaction time and fine motor coordination. We took his temperature, did an eye exam, and noted any strange feelings he reported.

Simon had a mild fever in the first hour. By the third hour, he had a productive cough, so we took regular samples of saliva and phlegm. He had labored breathing and a severe fever soon after. He reported having a mild headache and muscle aches.

Before he fell asleep he was still fully alert, but fatigued.

Julia installed an infusion port to take blood samples while he slept. I suggested that one of us stay with him at all times, so we scheduled shifts. I took the graveyard shift for the first night to let her sleep.

I recorded his temperature and heartrate through the night. His pulse was increasing, but he showed no signs of distress. His fever and flu-like symptoms gradually became more severe.

I spent the extra time trying to fix the incubator. It was especially important now, because there would be lots of living tissue to preserve when Simon died. I felt awful for thinking it, but it was a fact. Simon was giving his life to our research, and I was determined not to squander that gift.

I pulled out the digital thermostat and I didn't have the first clue how to fix it, but it gave me an idea. I took the broken part and ran to the faculty lounge.

I opened the front of the hot drink dispenser, removed the water tank and drink powders, and found the thermostat above the heating unit in the back. *Yes!* But my excitement was cut short when I compared the parts and found the connectors weren't even similar. The one in the drink dispenser was mechanical, not digital. But the principle was the same, so I tried think of a way around the problem. I ultimately decided to take the whole drink dispenser back to the lab.

Simon sprang up suddenly before dawn, vomiting in the eyewash station. I rushed to his side, but he jerked away.

"Where am I?" He was drenched in sweat, struggling against his restraints. "What are you doing to me?"

"Simon, it's okay. You're in the science lab."

His eyes darted around the room wildly. "Who are you? How did I get here?" The parasites were invading his brain, erasing everything he was before.

"I'm Max Hartwell. You got bit, and volunteered to let us observe you. You volunteered!" I held my hands up.

He looked in my eyes with a terrified expression, but then he recognized me. "You're Max. I'm Simon. We're in Thornhaven." He relaxed, breathing heavily. "I'm okay."

I cleaned him up, took vomit samples, and fed him some canned milk to calm his stomach. I offered him pain meds, but he refused, insisting that they be saved for Companions who needed them more. He really was a remarkable man.

When he was ready, I conducted the cognitive tests. His performance was slower and he seemed more distracted. He scored much lower on memory retention. I read him a short story and asked him to remember the details a few minutes later, and I read him some numbers and asked him to repeat them, adding a number to the list each round. He got half the score from his first round of tests, and was so frustrated he refused to continue.

After he fell back asleep, I examined slides of all our samples for evidence of the parasite. The phlegm had the same egg sacs and larva Julia found in the living lung tissue, which was no surprise. Simon's cough would transmit the same airborne infection we all carried. The adult parasites steadily increased in Simon's blood, confirming Julia's theory that blood contact transmits the adult parasite, not the egg sacs, but I also found adult parasites in Simon's saliva, and the highest concentration in his vomit. Simon's bites were already infectious, even though he hadn't changed.

When Julia arrived shortly after the morning bell, I was examining slides of my own blood and saliva to be sure there was no trace of the adult parasite. Julia said she'd convinced the Leadership Committee to suspend our regular work detail so we could spend more time with Simon. I explained everything I'd observed.

Finding the adult parasite in his vomit suggested that his digestive tract was infested, not just his brain. The parasite was probably preparing for its first meal.

"Why'd you take the coffeemaker out of the faculty lounge?" she asked.

"Let me show you!" I beamed. I opened the front panel and showed her the space inside, loaded with a tray of slides.

"You built a new incubator?"

"Exactly right!" I replied. "The temperature controls are less precise, so it took some tweaking to get it in the right range, but the heating unit does the job. It's also got a variable speed motor in the mixing chamber. It's designed for powdered drinks, but it'll mix anything we put in there."

"That's amazing!" She paused and looked concerned. "Max, did you tell anyone you were doing this?"

"No, why?"

"Well, right now the faculty lounge is full of confused companions looking for their morning coffee."

"Oh, right." I hadn't thought of that. "I just..."

"Don't even worry about it," she interrupted. "I'll take full responsibility. I'll convince them that the research required it. They can find another way to boil water." She smiled. "You've had a long night. Why don't you get some sleep. I can take over from here."

Chapter Thirty-Eight: Confession

Despite the attack, the Common Corps came home from S-Mart with packs bursting with supplies. Usually, Runners scavenged in two teams of two to cover more ground, but when a team reported that S-Mart had more supplies than they could carry, Nap led an eight-man squad to bring back as much as possible. They brought back duffle bags full of food, which was desperately needed. They also brought back tools: hammers, screwdrivers, saws, nails. As the building fell into disrepair, it was increasingly difficult to fix things without the proper supplies. Lightbulbs were hard to come by. The tools also helped the Safe Spaces crew dismantle outside structures and reinforce the fences, which were becoming more like walls.

They brought back enough soap that by cutting each bar into thirds, there was enough for everyone to have their own piece. I couldn't wait to wash my hair. After weeks of showering with only cold water, my hair was grimy and oily from sweat and smoke. It was funny that luxuries we took for granted before the collapse were now like gold.

Moses shot a moose while gathering firewood, and combined with the S-Mart supplies, people began to whisper about a feast. Whispers became rumors, rumors became plans, and before long, arrangements were being made without going through the Abundance committee. The idea swept through Thornhaven and was acted upon without permission. By the next General Assembly, the fact of the celebration was given, and people made proposals about decorations, and side dishes. The momentum of the feast was unstoppable. Miss Styx even tried to imply it was the Leadership Committee's idea. The feast was scheduled for the next Thursday.

Someone mentioned Thanksgiving, and it occurred to me that I'd turned twelve. My birthday was November twelfth. After all that had happened, it slipped my mind. Living day-to-day with so little to look forward to, I'd stopped paying attention to the date.

I went to the science lab and Julia had dimmed the lights. Simon was asleep.

"How is he doing?" I asked.

"Not good," Julia whispered. "His eyes and ears are painfully sensitive. That's why I dimmed the lights. His fever is worse and his heart's racing. Plus, he's constantly saying he's hungry, but he throws everything up."

"What about mentally?" I whispered.

"Hard to say. He comes and goes. Most of the time, he's too delusional for the tests. When he's lucid, he's too confused to follow the instructions. He's paranoid, and he doesn't seem to know where he is. When he got aggressive, I sedated him, and then strapped him down to this table." She pushed her clipboard in front of me. "But this is the bad news."

The page was filled with values measuring the composition of the blood samples. "What am I looking at?"

"Well, there's plenty to speculate about, but his acetylcholine level drops more every hour."

"What's acetylcholine?"

"A neurotransmitter, one of the common ones."

"What's a neurotransmitter?" I asked.

"It's a chemical that sends signals between brain cells. Acetylcholine is required for muscle coordination."

"You mean it keeps the mind communicating with the body?"

"Yeah. It also regulates heartrate, which could explain his rapid pulse. It's essential to the formation and retrieval of memories. Alzheimer's disease is an acetylcholine deficiency. It also promotes REM sleep, so the deficiency could explain the insomnia. And it contributes to impulse control, so a deficiency could promote aggressive behavior."

"So can we treat it? Where does acetylcholine come from?"

"Diet, mostly. Milk, eggs, whole wheat, but he throws up whatever he eats."

"Anywhere else?"

"Well, the best dietary source is meat... especially internal organs."

"Wait, what are you saying?" I asked.

"I'm saying if we feed it..."

"*Him*," I interrupted. "He's still a *him*."

She nodded. "If he eats enough acetylcholine-dense protein, and keeps it down, it may stall his mental and physical deterioration. But I don't know for how long, or what other damage the parasites are doing."

"It sounds like you're making some assumptions."

"Not assumptions," she responded. "I'm forming a hypothesis. We just don't have the resources to test it."

"What's that wonderful smell?" Simon was awake.

"What smell?" I asked.

"I don't know. It's everywhere." He closed his eyes and leaned his head back. "I'm so hungry." He panted in quick, shallow breaths.

Julia rushed to his side. "Simon, do you know where you are?"

"I should have stopped it! Something is wrong with me." Simon laughed hysterically. "It's me! I'm always so stupid!"

"Simon, what are you saying?" I asked.

"It's too late!" He practically growled as he pulled against his restraints. "I never wanted to hurt anybody!"

"Simon, you haven't hurt anybody," I said. "We won't let you hurt anybody."

"He's delirious," said Julia. "His fever is one hundred and seven, and his heart's about to explode."

"I have an idea!" I ran to the exit.

"Wait! Where are you going?"

I ran to the cafeteria where volunteers were preparing the feast. Moses was butchering the moose into manageable cuts of meat.

"Moses, I need meat!"

"Doh tink so. Is nah ready. I cookin up dis meat for de feas."

"Not that. Like, internal organs, whatever you're throwing away," I insisted.

"No Suh! I doh trow way nottin. I does use everyting fuh someting."

"Please! It's for Simon," I begged.

164

Moses stopped cutting. "Fella, you tell me what yuh need. Ah do anyting to help Simon."

Moses cut me a big slab of raw moose liver and wrapped it in newspaper. I ran back to the lab, where Simon was convulsing and pulling against his restraints.

"She's dead already!" he screamed.

"Get over here and help me!" Julia ordered. "We need to sedate him."

I ran toward them, but halted when Simon broke the straps on one arm and knocked Julia to the ground. He sat up and glared at me, his pupils constricted as he eyed the package in my hand. The blood had soaked through the newspaper and covered my hand. He snarled, reaching for me with his free arm.

I threw the package in his lap and stood back. He held it to his nose and breathed deep before devouring it. He didn't even unwrap it, and bit right through the paper. When he finished, he threw his head back—his hand and face covered with blood—grunted with relief, and collapsed on the lab station.

Julia crawled up to him, tied his arm back down, and injected his shoulder with a syringe of green liquid. "What was that?"

"Liver," I answered.

Simon sobbed loudly. "Kill me," he whimpered. "Have mercy."

"Who's dead already, Simon?" I asked.

"I don't know! She was just a girl," he cried. "How can we remember the dead if we don't even know their names?"

Julia and I exchanged a disturbed glance.

"We weren't ambushed. We attacked them!" He let out a deep sigh. "There was a group at S-Mart. Families. Why not trade with them, I asked, or bring them back with us. Make us stronger. No. Sheriff Nap said they were a threat. Said we couldn't trust them. Said we had to raid them while they weren't expecting it."

He continued. "We were hiding outside when she found us. Had to be only six or seven. If we let her go, he said, 'she'll blow our cover.'" He began gasping for air. "'We don't kill the living', I said, but he ordered me. I didn't want to kill her! I didn't want to hurt anybody!"

Simon wracked with violent seizures, convulsing uncontrollably. Julia and I held him down until it passed. He looked into my eyes. "We can't do things like this. If we do, we're no better than the dead ones. You have to forgive me… you have to make sure… have to…"

He went still, and I watched the life drain from his face.

"His heart stopped," reported Julia, taking her hands off him, and backing away.

Simon was gone.

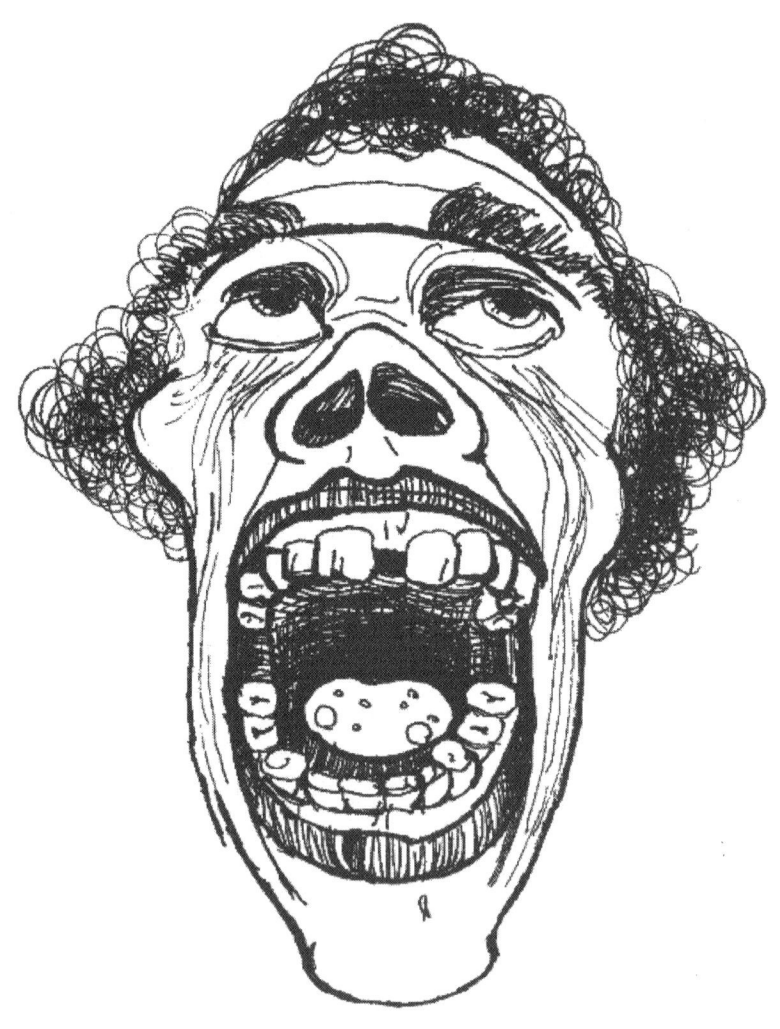

Chapter Thirty-Nine: Thanksgiving

Julia and I agreed not to tell people what Simon said until after Thanksgiving, so we didn't ruin the celebration. She'd bring it directly to the Leadership Committee in a private meeting to avoid alarming people.

Volunteers spent the day transforming the cafeteria into a banquet. They opened boxes delivered by the Common Corps and unloaded bag after bag of freeze-dried meals. Beef, potatoes, pasta, teriyaki chicken, egg and sausage breakfasts. Fruit mixes, drink mixes, dessert mixes. They were overwhelmed by all the choices. It seemed like Thornhaven would never go hungry again.

They boiled water from the well to prepare the freeze-dried packs as side dishes. Moses prepared a moose roast from the meatiest part of the rump. The smell of cooking meat and garlic filled the school hours before dinner was served.

Everyone, no matter how much they hated their job, was chipper and eager to put in a full day's work. When the final bell rang, everyone crowded at the cafeteria doors. Nap excused the Watchers on duty so they could eat with the whole community.

Moses beamed as he opened the doors and people rushed in.

Volunteers had secretly covered the cafeteria with handmade decorations. If there was anything Thornhaven had in actual abundance, it was art supplies. Orange construction paper was cut into pumpkins, turkeys made from the handprints of the younger kids, and autumn leaves strewn about like confetti and hung like streamers.

Volunteers scooped mashed potatoes with gravy made from the moose giblets, mixed vegetables, and tomato basil soup. Moses carved the roast himself, with more than enough to give everyone a hearty portion. They served a powdered orange drink, and it was all topped off with whipped cream and canned peaches for dessert.

As always, he Common Corps were served first, but rather than start eating, they sang the Anthem of Thornhaven. The whole room joined in, belting out the words in joyful unison.

We Companions, We Companions,
Stand together by the pyre,
And enjoy common salvation
In the safety of the brier.

In the valley, of the mountain,
Fight together in the wreath
To defend our fields of Thornton
From the forest's hands and teeth.

For our haven we will struggle.
Work together, never tire.
Equal rights and equal duties.
Peace among us, in the Shire.

Once everyone was seated, Miss Styx insisted on telling the story of the first Thanksgiving at Plymouth Colony, about the Pilgrims and Puritans who owed their first good harvest to the generosity of the indigenous peoples.

I always resented being taught this story. It wasn't true. There was no record of a "first good harvest" at Plymouth Colony. In fact, more than half the colonists starved to death in the first year. They never include the part of the story where treaties were broken and the natives were slaughtered. Not to mention, it wasn't declared a holiday until more than two hundred years later. The truth was that Abraham Lincoln invented Thanksgiving to foster unity after the Civil War. The gratitude that the colonists showed the natives was almost entirely a lie.

Moses was next. "Today is a rel blessin fuh Thornhaven. Is more dan juss some bacchanal to remembah some ol Tanksgivin feas that probably never happen. We celebratin we own harves, and getting ready for we own winta. We rememberin dose we lost, and we tankful for all we build. But dat's not de only way we like dose colonists. We standin at de edge of an undiscovered country. Yes, it frightenin. Yes, it dangerous. But we got de chance to begin de world over again. Wit no bigotry. Wit no genocide. Wit no tyranny or slavery. So, when allyuh eatin, rememba dat we got each udda to tank for dis meal. We all contributed to de prosperity of dis camp, and we all did our part to make dis meal possible. We provin dat de Earth still belongs to de livin, and not de dead, and we go take it back!"

The crowd exploded in applause, punching their fists in the air and pounding their utensils on the table, but I couldn't ignore that the food, except the roast, was stolen. I couldn't blame Moses. He didn't know. But Nap knew, and the Common Corps knew, laughing as they ate. Julia knew, but she smiled and boasted about our findings with Mrs. Mills. I wondered if it was wrong to be thankful for stolen food, food that was killed for.

I stood up. "Someone died for this food!" I yelled over the noise.

Everyone went silent. Nap stood up, staring me down with his creeper eye. It turned my guts upside down. He smiled and looked around the room.

"Max is right. It would be an injustice to eat without giving thanks to someone who gave their life so we could have this meal, someone who served with bravery and honor." He raised his glass of orange drink, and everyone raised theirs. "Simon," he paused, and then whispered to Miss Styx. "What was his last name?"

"Paige," she whispered.

"Simon Paige was bitten on the run to S-Mart, and he's no longer with us, but we do not forget our dead. Simon Paige has earned his place as a Martyr of Thornhaven. So today we drink to Simon, and all our fallen heroes."

The drink was sweet and tangy. Almost too sweet. It had been so long since I'd had processed sugar or candy that my sense of taste had changed. But it was bitter, too. All the food tasted bitter knowing it wasn't rightfully ours, except the moose.

"Now, a moment of silence," said Nap. "To honor our dead and remember all we're thankful for."

I scoffed. What was there to be thankful for in this mess? Dad was dead. My home was destroyed. The PorcScouts were missing. Ellie was dead for lack of basic antibiotics. Now I was stuck in this prison camp.

I forced myself to stop thinking that way. Holland and Staci were new friends. Even Scott wasn't so bad. We had heat and clean water. There were walls and men with guns defending them. I was safe, and that was more than most people had. Most people were creepers and I'd managed to avoid that fate.

Everyone ate until they were bursting. I had a second helping of the roast but I couldn't eat anything else. Everyone ate, drank, and laughed late into the evening.

When they were done, no one in the Common Corps was fit to keep watch so Moses volunteered. Nap agreed, seeing how he had proven he was a good shot.

Chapter Forty: Black Friday

"Max, knock it off."

I woke up in the dark. It was unusually cold.

"Quit it! I'm trying to sleep." It was Staci.

"Staci, you're dreaming. I'm not doing anything."

She went quiet, and I almost dozed off, but then I heard her eating something.

"Seriously! You're eating right now? Keep it down," said Holland.

I sat up, fished around my book bag for Ellie's flashlight, and clicked it on.

Moses was covered in blood, gnawing on Staci's feet, but she hadn't noticed.

"BREACH!" screamed Holland.

Staci bolted up and let out a nightmarish scream. She tried to pull herself away, but Moses had her, finishing her feet and biting into the meat of her calves.

Kids panicked, running into the hall, or out the back door into the night. Someone pulled the lockdown alarm.

I grabbed Moses's legs, Holland grabbed Staci's arms, and we pulled them apart. Staci sobbed and screamed.

"Guys! A little help?" I stopped pulling Moses and he twisted around and tried to grab me. If I let go, Moses would attack someone else, so I kept pulling its legs, dragging it on its belly so it couldn't get up.

"Hang on!" yelled Holland. "I saw this in a movie!" He blasted Moses in the face with a fire extinguisher. The air filled with white plumes as I let go and backed away.

When the mist settled, Moses was covered in white powder.

"What was that supposed to do?" I asked.

"It's CO_2. I thought it would freeze him," said Holland.

"Don't be stupid!"

It couldn't see and stumbled toward the sound of our voices, swiping at the air.

"Don't you rejects know anything?" Scott came through the fog with a fire ax. "You have to destroy the brain." He wound up, and when Moses turned toward his voice, he swung and embedded the ax in the side of its head. Moses dropped hard, gurgled and reached for Scott's foot. He stepped on its back, yanked out the ax, and dropped it on the creeper's neck, sending the head rolling across the floor.

"I'm dead! I'm so dead! Oh my God! Oh my God!" cried Staci.

I ran to her side, untied my shoe laces and started cinching her legs like a tourniquet.

"You're wasting your time." Scott raised the ax over his head. "I'll take care of it."

I jumped between Scott and Staci. "No! She's still alive!"

"The rules are simple. We got a zero-tolerance policy for undead geeks," Scott said.

Staci gulped mouthfuls of air and began losing consciousness. I'd never seen so much blood.

"There's still time," I insisted. "We take her to the nurse's office. The alarm will wake up Mrs. Mills. That's the first place she'll go. She'll know how to amputate."

The blood spread near Scott's feet and he backed away.

"That's the right move. That's what we're doing!" I ordered.

"Guys!" Holland had ripped open Moses's shirt and found a deep wound in his chest. "Moses was shot!"

"**W**hat do you mean shot?" yelled Scott.

"I mean shot. With a gun," responded Holland. "That doesn't make any sense."

"Guy's, it doesn't matter how we die. We all change. Moses was on the roof last night. Whoever shot him let him loose down here on purpose." I was devastated that Moses was dead, but I didn't have even an instant to dwell on it. "Don't you get it? We're under attack! Now help me!"

Holland and I carried Staci into the hall while Scott covered us with the ax. Kids pounded on classroom doors, looking for the adults. People woken up by the lockdown alarm came out in the hall, looking confused. It's amazing how quickly people forget their training in a real emergency. Runners were supposed to go to the roof. Watchers were supposed to man gun ports throughout the school. Nap was supposed to go to the security office. Mrs. Mills was supposed to go to the nurse's office. And everyone else was either supposed to lock their rooms or get to the library. None of that was happening.

We took Staci to the nurse's office, and laid her on an examination table. I cradled her head, my hands covered in blood. Her breathing was shallow, her pulse was weak, and Mrs. Mills wasn't at her post.

"What now?" asked Holland, his voice full of desperation.

"We cut off her legs," insisted Scott.

"We can't!" I resisted. "She'll bleed out! We have to wait for Mrs. Mills."

"Good morning S-Mart shoppers!" A voice came over the PA system. Someone was in the security office, but it wasn't Nap. "But you're not really shoppers, are you? You're shoplifters." It was Major Winters.

"Oh crap!" I said.

173

"I bet you didn't think you'd be hearing this voice again. You may have noticed that poor old Moses has suffered a work-related injury. I'm shocked you people only left one man on watch. We're going to need a clean-up on aisle, well, wherever he ended up. I see you've altered the surveillance system since I left. Makes my job difficult." He laughed.

"Now that I have your attention I'd like to clear the air. We parted on such bad terms. It was wrong to kill Officer Pike. I see that now. To be honest, I was afraid. I thought without the Capitol calling the shots, people like you wouldn't need people like me. But my new family helped me understand that the world will always need people of my unique skill set. We'll always need order, and structure, security and regiment. My new family embraces that. They've taken me in. Lifted me up. Throw me to the dogs and I come back Alpha of the pack." He howled into the mic. "Am I right?"

"Guys, look at this!" yelled Scott.

The examination room had a gun port drilled into the boards covering the rear window. It was only large enough for a rifle barrel. The dawn light was just enough to see men surrounding the building. They were dressed in light blue S-Mart uniforms, and taking cover in the playground and refugee tents.

"I don't like the looks of this," Holland said.

"How could I refuse when they asked for my help dealing with some sloppy band of amateur bandits and their potbellied old Sheriff who killed their people and raided their pantry?" said Winters. "You rookies didn't even cover your tracks."

"What the heck is he talking about?" asked Holland.

"We're under attack," I answered.

"By who?"

"S-Mart."

"I want you to know that this is nothing personal between us," the Major continued. "Heck, it wasn't even my idea. I'm just enforcing the will of the majority. It's funny; in basic training they told us democracies don't go to war with each other, but that's not even remotely true if one democracy plunders another." He paused.

"Now, we're not unreasonable people. We've got deal for you, a Black Friday special. You give us back what you stole, turn over Sheriff Nap to answer for his crimes, throw in whatever medical supplies you've got laying around, and we walk away. Think of it as restitution for our injuries, and blowback for your poor choice of leadership. You cooperate, nothing goes down. Resist us, and we go door buster clearance sale on this place. You've got five minutes."

Holland looked panicked. "What the heck do we do now?"

"Fight or flee," answered Scott.

"What about Staci?" I insisted. "We have to… "

"She's dead either way," Scott interrupted. "Even if we did it ourselves, we don't have time to close the wound."

"Guys!" Holland checked Staci's pulse. "She's gone."

"What!?" I checked for myself. No breathing. No pulse. "No!" I started chest compressions.

Scott and Holland backed away slowly. "How long?" Holland asked.

I stopped. "It's different for everyone," I whispered.

"Call me crazy," Holland continued, "but I don't wanna be here when it happens."

I pulled a sheet over Staci's body.

"What the heck are you doing?" asked Scott. "We don't got time for a ceremony."

"They're coming for medical supplies, right? Well, I want to give her a chance to catch them off guard when they do."

"That's dark," said Scott. "I like it."

"Hey!" Holland interrupted. "This is a guard post, right?" We both nodded. "Shouldn't there be a weapon here?"

"No," I said. "Everyone in the Kill Squad is issued a firearm. The rest are locked in the Armory. But there should be a radio!"

We searched and found the police radio. I scanned the dial for chatter before turning to the channel used by the Kill Squad.

"This is a HERD report from the nurse's station. We got six breathers with long guns, in S-Mart uniforms, taking cover behind the school. Are there any other active guard posts? Over."

A few moments later, a voice broke in. "Hello? I'm here. Uh, am I using this right? This is Mr. Ash. I'm in the cafeteria with some others. We're okay. What's going on?"

"It's not a cellphone. We can only speak one at a time, and you have to say 'over' when you're done," I explained. "Are you armed? Over."

"Oh, sorry. Uh, let me check." Silence. "Yeah, we have a shotgun here. Over."

"You should be able to see the front of the school from there. Give me a HERD report. Over."

"There's an S-Mart truck outside the gate. Like a big box truck. Men with rifles, and something... oh my God! The truck is full of biters!"

Chapter Forty-Two: Hide and Seek

"Time's up, folks. If you won't give me Nap, we're gonna have to play a little game of Hide and Seek."

There was a huge crash and peppering of gunfire outside. Someone from Thornhaven was firing back. "They broke through the front gate!" Mr. Ash screamed on the radio. "Guys, they're coming in!"

"Time to move!" Scott grabbed the radio from me. "You two get to the library. Radio me when you get there."

"Where are you going?" I asked.

"I'm going after the Major." He ran off with the ax and the radio.

"Scott, wait!" but he was gone.

"It's a no brainer," said Holland. "They've got a shotgun and a view in the cafeteria. We've got a sleeping monster. Let's go there."

"You go. I'll catch up. I have to grab something."

PorcScouts Rule #23, *It's better to have your gear and not need it, than need your gear and not have it.*

I ducked into the locker room on the way to the cafeteria. It was dark, and empty. I opened my locker and threw everything on the floor to get to the hidden compartment. I grabbed my gear bag. I had food, water, medical supplies, P.E. clothes, Dad's radio, and some other gear.

I threw the bag over my shoulders and moved toward the exit when the doorknob turned and the hinges creaked.

"Did you hear that?" said a male voice.

"Yeah. Someone is in here," answered a female voice.

They were unfamiliar, but the gurgles and snarls that followed were clear. They had a creeper with them.

I backed away from the door, and went down a row of lockers out of sight.

The woman swept through the shower stalls with her rifle, calling out, "Clear!" for each one. The man had the creeper. The steps of his boots were deliberate, and quiet, while the creeper's were more of an awkward shuffle. They were moving closer and closer.

I had to hide, fast. I climbed inside my locker and closed the door except a crack. If I let it latch, I'd be trapped inside.

The man had the creeper by the neck with a robotic claw and metal arm, like an animal handler might use. The creeper was an old woman. I recognized her. She was the S-Mart greeter before the collapse. All three of them wore S-Mart uniforms.

He walked down the row, pointing the creeper along the lockers, under benches, and anywhere someone might hide. It sniffed like a police dog, passing over the clean clothes bin, but taking interest in the dirty clothes bin.

Why wasn't it attacking them? Why did it cooperate? Had they trained it somehow? Did creepers respect uniforms for some reason? The Postman at Lochshire wore a uniform. Maybe that's part of why the others followed it. Was that possible?

The creeper snorted and growled, pulling its handler forward.

"Charlie, come quick!" called the man. "Lucy found something."

They followed the creeper to my locker.

He kicked my stuff on the ground. "Someone was in here. Maybe they left."

Charlie readied her rifle and pointed it at my locker, which I'd left slightly open. "Collin, open it up. I'll cover you," she whispered.

Collin wrapped his pudgy fingers around the locker door and I slammed it on him. He screamed and yanked his hand back, cursing, and I pulled the locker closed.

Charlie tried the locker door, but it had latched. They were locked out, but I was locked in. She pressed her eye up to the ventilation holes in the locker door to try to see in. "You just made a serious mistake, you little stain. We got you now!"

I ripped down the map and squeezed through the hole into the other locker and tried to disengage the broken lock with my multi-tool, but it was no use.

Charlie pounded on the lock with the butt of her rifle over and over. Collin screamed, "You're going to pay for that, Kid."

The words kept repeating in my head, *You're inside, not outside. You're inside, not outside.* Like a riddle I knew, but just couldn't answer.

178

Charlie fired the rifle, and the blast was deafening inside the locker. She'd blown off the lock. My ears were ringing; I could hardly hear anything.

Suddenly, it occurred to me that the hinges were on the inside of the locker. I wedged the flathead screwdriver on my multi-tool into to the top of the first hinge and dug out the pin, releasing the hinge.

Collin opened the other locker. "What the heck? Grab him!" He charged into the locker, but he was too fat to get through.

I pried out the second pin and the door came off its hinges. It was still locked on the other side, but it was loose enough that I could bust out and run for the exit.

"There he is!" yelled Collin. "Shoot him!"

"Don't be stupid. He's just a kid," replied Charlie. "Let Lucy have him!"

Collin released the metal grabber and Lucy came after me. I almost made it to the exit when Lucy tackled me. It wrestled me to the ground as I banged it into lockers. I struggled to keep its hands off me, but it took all my strength to push its mouth away.

Charlie and Collin watched and laughed.

I bashed Lucy's head into a bench, but it got its jaws around my hand and bit down. I screamed when my pinky cracked.

I kicked it off me. That didn't stop it, but it gave me enough time to scramble to the door.

Charlie trained her rifle on me, but Collin stopped her. "Let him go. He's not who we're looking for."

I burst into the hallway and slammed the door in Lucy's face. Everywhere I turned, there were teams with rifles, and creepers, all in S-Mart uniforms. A man gripped his bleeding arm while his partner fired into the nurse's office. Staci got him. Down the main hall, there was a firefight in front of the cafeteria. The Common Corps were defending the food. The gunfire was echoing throughout the halls.

The science wing was clear. I ran, thinking of the taser in the lab. I thought I'd lock myself inside, and push the freezer in front of the door. I thought I'd ambush anyone who broke in. But then my eye caught the exit sign at the end of the hall.

With so many of them inside, there couldn't be many left outside. Maybe they were distracted. Maybe there was cover fire. Whatever was out there, I'd break for the woods and find cover. Leave this whole ugly mess behind and get to the cabin. I slid to a full stop when the exit door swung open.

Sunlight poured in, nearly blinding me. When my eyes adjusted, terror sent me charging the other way. This S-Mart team weren't strangers—they were Freddy Wozzeck and Matt Cordell.

"What good fortune is this?" Matt took aim. "I got some payback for you, you little snot!" He took aim, fired, and missed.

Woz began his hysterical laughter.

If you're under fire and can't take cover, your only option is to make yourself a difficult target by running in odd angles and random patterns. My only hope for cover was a classroom, so I zigzagged from one side to the other, but all the doors were locked.

I pushed my legs until it felt like my muscles would tear. As I reached for the door to the lab, his next shot barely missed me and hit the doorknob. I darted across the hall and the next door was unlocked! His last shot hit the door as I pulled it open and ran inside.

I slammed the door and snapped the deadbolt. Matt jiggled the knob, and gave it three SWAT raid kicks before giving up. He opened fire, but the door was solid steel.

"There's no way out of there, Stupid!" yelled Matt as Woz continued laughing. "You gotta come out eventually, and when you do, we'll be gunning for you."

I caught my breath, and found myself in the boiler room.

Chapter Forty-Three: The Dungeon of the Unfortunates

My hand throbbed. It was soaking wet from Lucy's bite. I had to find a blade, or something, and shuddered at the thought of cauterizing it in the furnace. The boiler room was pitch-black. No windows. No lights. I tried the switch by the door, but got nothing.

I clicked Ellie's flashlight on and examined my hand. It was dripping with Lucy's putrid slobber, but there was no blood. I wiped it on my sweatpants and found no open wound. Lucy never broke the skin. It had no teeth! *Did the S-Mart people pull the teeth out of their creepers for their own safety?* My pinky was broken, but it would mend. I was searching my gear bag for the trauma kit, when I heard a familiar sound.

"Meeoow!"

"Stinky!?" He sounded desperate, frightened, and far away.

When he heard me, his cries came faster and louder. "Meow. Meow. Meow."

"I'm coming!" I shined my light down the stairs but couldn't see beyond the occasional glint of an air duct, or a pipe. The steps creaked as I pointed my tiny light into the darkness, and I moved toward the sound.

The smell hit me. Dank, stale corpses.

I moved into the glow of the furnace. It cast a warm, orange glow on a pile of chopped wood, and a heap of bodies. Most were creepers from outside, not Companions. Bins next to the furnace were labeled, "winter clothes," "weapons and gear," and "perishables." Behind them was a bulletin board covered with ID cards, newspaper clippings, old library cards, and whatever identifying information was in their pockets.

Stinky howled, but then I heard rattling of some kind. I shined my light toward it. There was a steel table where someone had placed a razor, a toothbrush, a copy of *The Trial of Dr. Frankenstein*, a rotary telephone, and a tape player.

181

A hulking figure grasped out of the darkness and into the furnace light, lunging across the table at me. I leapt back. It was Simon, fully transformed and chained to the wall. Its face was covered in blood. Someone had been feeding it.

"Meow!"

I turned toward the sound when the light caught the edge of another steel table, and another, and another. Three in all.

The body on the first table was covered in a white sheet; blood soaked through around the head. The covered body on the second table had blood drenching the mid-section. The body on the third table was under a sheet with a smaller blood stain on the arm.

I peeled back the first sheet. It was Andre. Someone had opened his skull and performed a crude exploratory brain surgery. Most of the neocortex was cut away, exposing the structures of the limbic system and reptilian brain below.

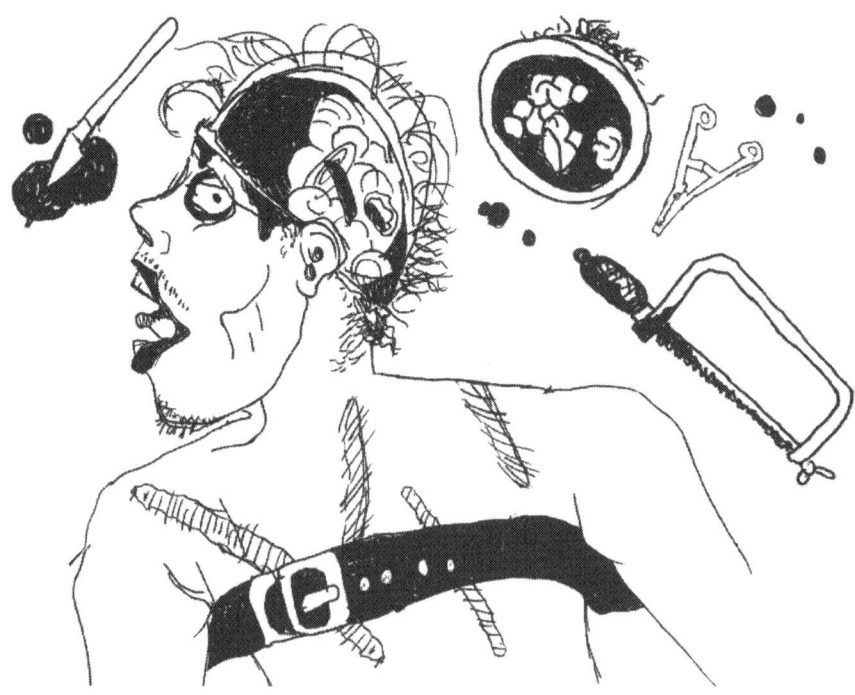

I gasped when its eyes opened and rolled toward me. Its jaw gabbed compulsively, but its body didn't twitch, as if it were disconnected.

I peeled back the second sheet; Livia. I could tell that her belly was flat but I didn't have the stomach to lift the shroud.

I approached the third table, but was distracted by a work area on the other side.

It looked like a makeshift autopsy lab. Forceps and scissors, scalpels and bone saws, dissection pans and T pins.

And Stinky.

He was on his side, and strapped to a large cookie sheet. Laid out next to him were a white towel, a spectrum of surgical tools, and a syringe of green liquid.

"Stinky! Who did this to you?" But I knew. Ms. Lessard finally caught her specimen. Whatever she was planning was interrupted by the lockdown alarm. I pulled the straps off him as he squirmed his way free. He leapt into my arms and I held him.

"Max?" The whisper was so faint I thought she was right behind me.

I spun around, clutching Stinky with one arm and pointing the light with the other, but no one was there.

The third body shifted beneath the sheet. It fell away and I saw her pale, weak body, with a bloody bite on her arm.

"Ellie!"

Chapter Forty-Four: Hot Air

"They told me you were dead!"

"They exaggerated," she whispered meekly.

I examined the bite. "What happened?" I felt her forehead, but there was no fever. "How fresh is it?"

"She used that thing." Ellie pointed at Simon. "Some kind of experiment." She pulled the sheet to cover herself.

"I'm an idiot. Put these on." I gave her the extra P.E. uniform. It was a little big for her. She had to roll the waistband to hold the sweatpants up, but it did the job.

She held my hand and examined my crooked finger. "Good old Max," she smiled weakly. "Prepared for everything." She pushed my hair out of my face and examined my injured ear. "Do you have any food?"

I opened my pack and let her take as much as she wanted. She grabbed a belt cheese and a bag of crackers. I teared up looking at the bite. "Why would she do this?"

"This is why." She pulled up a pant leg, where she had a ring of puncture scars. They were fully healed, and months old.

"Is that what I think it is?"

She nodded. "It's a bite. It happened in Boston."

"But that's impossible," I exclaimed.

"Max. I lied when I said my mom and I went north to find snow."

Private Woz's laughter echoed upstairs, followed by the jingle of keys.

I turned to Ellie. "There's some bad guys up there who are trying to kill me. Is there another way out of here?"

"I don't know. I don't think so."

Stinky leapt up on the work desk, and climbed onto a shelf next to it. I tried to grab him, but he was too high.

"Stinky! Come back!"

He stood on his hind legs on top of the shelf and reached as high as he could. He raked his claws against a grill on the bottom of an air duct. He looked down and meowed to get my attention, then went back to raking the vent.

"That's genius!"

I climbed up the shelf and pulled on the vent, but it was fastened with hex screws.

"Ellie, look for a hex wrench or a crowbar. Something I can force this open with."

She searched desk drawers and brought a toolbox to the edge of the furnace light. "Try this!" She handed me a strange stainless steel contraption. It had two horizontal arms connected by a vertical bar with teeth like a gear rack. One arm had a hand crank on the side.

"What is it?"

"A rib spreader."

Obviously. I looked at the grill of the vent. It did resemble ribs. I cranked the arms closed and wedged it in the vent. I spun the crank in reverse and gradually forced the vent open. Hot air hit me in the face.

In the dark, the deadbolt snapped and the hinges of the boiler room door squeaked.

"Max?" came Matt's voice. "Ready or not, here we come!"

I pushed the rib spreader as far as it would go. When the crank arm reached the end of the gear rack, it slipped off and dropped to the ground with a clang.

"Time to move," I whispered. "Get up here." I reached down.

"Go ahead. I have to get something." She ran into the dark.

"Wait!"

Stinky leapt into the duct and meowed for me to follow. I peered into the dark boiler room. "Ellie?"

The stairs creaked under heavy footfalls as Matt and Woz came down. "Did you hear that? He's down here somewhere," said Matt.

Ellie came back and started climbing.

"Get up here!" I pulled her up and helped her into the duct ahead of me. It was easy for Stinky, but narrow for me and Ellie. I couldn't fit with the gear bag. I had to tie it to my foot and drag it behind me.

"What did you grab?" I asked.

She turned around with a big grin and handed me a steel pin.

"What is it?"

Before she could answer I heard Matt's voice. "Is that Simon?" I heard Simon's chain fall to the ground. Matt screamed and gunshots rang out as Simon roared.

"You're amazing!" I told her.

She smiled. "I know."

"Meow." Stinky ran a few feet ahead and turned back. "Meow!" He circled in place and meowed again.

"What's with him?" Ellie asked.

"I think he knows the way. He wants us to follow him."

Stinky lead us through the labyrinth of air ducts, running ahead and turning back to meow when we fell behind. It was a long, hard crawl. It was tight, and the hot air was hard to breathe.

Stinky stopped at an intersection that was lit from above. He meowed to make sure we were watching and leapt up.

The opening was the turbine vent that was demolished when the Major crashed the helicopter. Stinky peered down the hole at us, looking proud.

"That must be how he got in!" I exclaimed.

"What do you mean?" Ellie asked.

"All the doors and windows in the school are locked or boarded up. Stinky must have used the air ducts to get around this whole time." I boosted Ellie up. "Do you see anything?"

She poked her head out and looked around. "I don't see anyone. Everyone must be inside."

I pushed her feet up and she climbed out. I handed my gear bag up.

She reached down. "Come on. I'll help you up."

"Just a minute. I think I see something." I shined my light through a nearby vent and saw the Sig Sauer Mosquito I'd hidden. I pushed on the grate, but it was screwed on the other side.

I braced myself against the side of the intersection and kicked the grate. After three kicks, a screw tore free and one corner pushed in. Three more kicks on the other side and it popped off.

186

I reached in and grabbed the gun. It was small, but better than nothing. It was still loaded with ten .22LR rounds.

"Who the hell is making that noise?" It was the Major in the room below me.

Scuffles and mumbles came from someone who sounded gagged.

"Pipe down in here or I will feed you to the meat puppets!" He paused, and spoke into a radio. "Woz, this is Winters. Have you found the last brat yet? Let's wrap this up."

The door closed as the Major went back in the art room.

I pulled a white panel out of the drop ceiling and peered down. Holland and Scott were bound and gagged, sitting on the floor against the empty shelf. Holland saw me and started squirming and moaning. I held my finger to my lips to silence him and climbed down.

Their wrists and ankles were bound with thick plastic zip ties. I cut them with the knife on my multi-tool.

"Be very quiet," I whispered. "Climb up, and get into the air duct. Then climb up to the roof through the skylight. We're getting out of here for good." I pulled out their gags. "Hurry!"

"What about him?" Holland pointed and I spun around.

Nap was sitting on the cot across the room, bound and gagged. He moaned and turned around so I could cut his wrists. I pulled the knife again and moved toward him, but stopped.

"Wait." I backed away, holding the knife more defensively. "You did this."

He glared at me.

"You attacked S-Mart. You lead them back here. This is your fault."

He screamed into his gag for me to untie him.

"You lied to us. You stole food. And you killed the living. That's three strikes, Sheriff."

His eyes went wide, and his creeper eye burned into me. My heart pounded as I stared back. He rolled on his back and started kicking the door and screaming.

"Go, go, go," I ordered to Holland and Scott as we climbed the shelf.

"Don't make me come in there and beat the wind out of you!" the Major yelled through the door.

Holland and Scott were through the grate. The Major burst into the room just as I put the ceiling panel back in place.

"Where the hell are they?" he screamed.

I climbed into the duct.

We crawled to the skylight where Stinky was meowing frantically. I helped Scott and Holland up; then Scott pulled me up.

My gear bag was there, but Ellie was gone. "Ellie?" I looked around, but didn't see her.

"Where's Ellie?" I began to panic.

"Who?" asked Scott.

Holland shrugged.

"Ellie!" I yelled, to no response.

Chapter Forty-Five: Dr. Frankenstein

I scanned the rooftop and didn't see her. On the far side, smoke billowed out of the building. The cafeteria was on fire. I ran to the edge and scanned the zip line, thinking maybe she went down ahead of me. The S-Mart group had crashed their box truck through the front gates and let their creepers loose inside. The gunfire and smoke attracted more. The yard was swarming with creepers again, but there were no people. The S-Mart group must have gone inside.

"Max!" I heard her scream and spun around.

Ms. Lessard came out from behind the helicopter, clutching Ellie by the neck. "Not one step closer!" she yelled, pressing a scalpel to Ellie's throat. "You and your friends, grab your gear and hit the road, but this one stays with me."

"We're not leaving without her!" I felt the pistol in my pocket. "Let her go!"

"Not a chance! She's too important."

"Open your eyes! Thornhaven has fallen. The Major has won. It's over!"

She scoffed. "You really think I care who wins this stupid war? I'm a scientist! Science doesn't pick sides. It's just the living and the dead. It doesn't matter if this place is run by the Major or the Sheriff, S-Mart or Thornhaven. We'll put out the fires and close it up again. Then it's back to business, and this lovely specimen is the key to solving this plague. You, of all people, should recognize that."

"You're insane! You really think they'll let you keep doing your experiments when they find that torture chamber down there?"

She laughed. "They who? The Sheriff knows. The Major knows. Nurse Mills and Miss Styx know. You think I snuck all that equipment in without any help? Lots of people support what I'm doing, because they know what's at stake."

"Yeah, well I don't support it!" I pulled out the Mosquito and aimed at her. "And I'm calling the shots. Now, let her go."

"Max, we both know you're not going to shoot me. You're too good. You're missing the bigger picture. We are facing human extinction. Sometimes, the few must be sacrificed so the majority can survive. We're talking about a cure! We could put the world back the way it was. You should help! How can you be so selfish?"

"If you believed she was so important, you wouldn't be threatening to hurt her."

"Oh, I don't know." She grinned. "I've studied her immunity to bites pretty thoroughly. It might be medically relevant to see if she's immune to reanimation after death. An autopsy would certainly be revealing. Who knows? Killing her might be just the breakthrough we need." She pressed the scalpel to Ellie's neck until she screamed. "Now drop the gun!"

Ellie looked at me with pleading eyes and nodded. "Do it," she mouthed. She had a plan. Whatever it was, I was going to play along.

"You're right." I raised my hands and pointed the gun in the air. "Just don't hurt her."

"Good. Now, throw it over there." She motioned toward the helicopter with the scalpel, taking it off Ellie's neck for an instant.

Ellie swung her elbow up, hitting Ms. Lessard in the nose. While she was stunned, Ellie drew a syringe from her waistband and plunged it in Ms. Lessard's neck.

It was the anesthetic that Ms. Lessard had prepped for Stinky.

Ms. Lessard stumbled back, blood pouring from her nose and throat, slashing the scalpel at nothing.

Ellie ran to me and I turned toward Ms. Lessard. Scott and Holland stood behind me as we watched the sedative take effect.

Ms. Lessard fixed her eyes on me, took two steps forward, stumbled to the side and fell over the edge of the building.

We ran to the edge and looked down.

She landed near a pack of creepers that were beating on the front entrance. For a moment, she was on her feet and moving away, but promptly stumbled and fell flat on her face. She started crawling away on her hands and knees. The creepers were slow, but so was she. The first creeper caught the hem of her dress, and as it wrestled with her, it sank its teeth in her shoulder. She screamed until it gnawed through her neck, and her voice was choked with blood. Creepers shambled toward her from all directions, and within moments, the herd had overtaken her.

"Show's over, guys. We're wasting daylight," said Scott.

"He's right. We can't stay here," agreed Holland. "But where can we go?"

"I know a place," I answered.

Scott went down the zip line first, followed by Holland. Ellie went ahead of me and I went last, with Stinky riding in my gear bag.

Chapter Forty-Six: Denton's Sugar Shack

We needed shelter, fast. No one was dressed for snow, and Ellie wasn't even wearing shoes. In freezing temperatures, hypothermia and frostbite can take effect in less than ten minutes. I lead the group to a little café in town called Denton's Sugar Shack, less than a mile south of Thornhaven. Dad used to bring me there for pancakes on cold mornings. It was a wooden cabin, which was all we could hope for. It was secure, as long as no one found us.

I built a fire immediately from paper and broken wooden chairs. Thankfully, Holland still had matches in his digital camera case. Everyone was shivering, and I could feel the numbness creeping over my fingers. Ellie had actually stopped shivering, and she had complained of a prickling feeling in her fingers and toes—early symptoms of frostbite.

The advertisement out front read, "The best maple syrup in New Hampshire." I don't know if that was true, but there was nothing left in the pantry. Everything within three miles of Thornhaven had already been looted. We ate rat meat and melted snow.

No one spoke. Ellie seemed far away.

I tried to break the ice. "Have you ever noticed almost every superhero is an orphan?"

Silence.

"Spiderman was raised by his aunt," I continued. "Batman was raised by his butler. Superman's whole planet was destroyed. Harry Potter was raised by that weird family."

"Luke Skywalker," whispered Holland. "Leia, too. They're twins."

"What's your point?" asked Scott

"I was just thinking, the whole world is orphans now. Maybe the whole world is full of heroes?"

"And villains," added Scott. "Magneto. Darth Vader. Dr. Evil."

"There is that," I agreed.

"Guys." Holland was staring at his cracked reading glasses. "I don't want to be Holland anymore. I never really was."

"I knew it!" exclaimed Scott. "You're Niles aren't you?"

Niles nodded and put the glasses on.

"But why?" asked Scott.

"I don't know. I just thought," he looked up, eyes full of tears. "If everyone thought I was him, it was like he wasn't really dead, and as long as I knew the truth, I wasn't really dead, either. I know, it sounds so stupid."

"I don't think it's stupid, Niles," I said.

Ellie spoke without looking up from the fire. "The first time I was bitten was in Boston. When nothing happened, Mom kept it secret, but the military found the bite during their house-to-house medical examinations. They airlifted me to a research facility at the FEMA camp in Manchester. Lab rats got treated better than me. Blood tests, brain scans, biopsies. They didn't know what they were searching for so they looked everywhere. They kept talking about my brain. They said I had unique architecture. They flew in some kind of expert, a brain surgeon. That's when Mom busted us out."

"Why go north?" I asked.

"Your Dad," she answered. "My mom knew him from before. She thought he could figure it out. Even if he couldn't, she knew we'd be safe with him."

"Oh..."

"When the school nurse saw my scar, she turned me over to Ms. Lessard. The Sheriff helped her set the lab up and keep it secret. The Major looked for new equipment, and brought her test subjects. Once she confirmed I was immune to bites, she started testing the strength of my immunity. She injected my blood in a creeper, but nothing changed. She injected creeper blood into me and when nothing happened, she forced me to eat it. Every time they found new equipment, she devised some new experiment. A new way of measuring. A new vector for infection. She would have killed me."

"I'm so sorry," I said. "They told me you were dead."

"It's not your fault. I'm just glad we're out of there."

"Speaking of which," interrupted Scott, "seems to me we need a plan. I don't feel like starving to death in an empty restaurant and I'm not going back to that school, no matter who's in charge."

I looked at Ellie and our new companions. "The plan hasn't changed. We'll spend the night. I've got enough breakfast for all of us. In the morning, we head to my cabin, and scavenge for food and weapons on the way. I'll get us there. I promise!"

END PART II

Made in the USA
Columbia, SC
17 October 2017